ALSO BY PATRICK JONES

STOLEN CAR

PATRICK JONES

Walker & Company
New York

To JLJ

First published in the United States of America in 2008 by Walker Publishing Company, Inc.
Visit Walker & Company's Web site at www.walkeryoungreaders.com

For information about permission to reproduce selections from this book, write to
Permissions, Walker & Company, 175 Fifth Avenue, New York, New York 10010

Library of Congress Cataloging-in-Publication Data
Jones, Patrick.
Stolen car / Patrick Jones.—1st ed.
p.   cm.
Summary: Fifteen-year-old Danielle desperately wants to escape life with her mother and a series of "Dad-
wannabes," so when best friends Ashley and Evan help her see that bad-boy Reid is lying and using her,
Danny steals Reid's car and takes Ashley on a road trip.
ISBN-13: 978-0-8027-9700-1 • ISBN-10: 0-8027-9700-8
[1. Mothers and daughters—Fiction. 2. Family problems—Fiction. 3. Best friends—Fiction.
4. Friendship—Fiction. 5. Automobile driving—Fiction. 6. Single-parent families—Fiction.
7. Flint (Mich.)—Fiction.] I. Title.
PZ7.J7242Sto 2008   [Fic]—dc22   2008000253

Book design by Daniel Roode
Typeset by Westchester Book Composition
Printed in the U.S.A. by Quebecor World Fairfield
2 4 6 8 10 9 7 5 3 1

All papers used by Walker & Company are natural, recyclable products made
from wood grown in well-managed forests. The manufacturing processes
conform to the environmental regulations of the country of origin.

ACKNOWLEDGMENTS

Stolen Car was test-driven by teenagers in New York, Connecticut, Michigan, Ohio, Wisconsin, and Minnesota. In particular, I want to acknowledge the following students from Hudson High School in Hudson, Wisconsin, who helped me: Zach Reams, Jesse Griem, Mike Heth, Kelsey Bosman, Leah Glodowski, Shelbi Ball, Bailey Boron, Lisa LaBeau, Madalyn Gibson, Maddie Karras, Maggie Whitacre, MacKenzee Nicely, Allison Hawthorne, Beth Tiedemann, and Bradley Lindberg. Also thanks to other teens who lent me their eyes: Allison from Minnesota, Samantha aka Lolly Dreamer from the Creek in Michigan, as well as Gabby and Meredith from Connecticut. Also thanks to the "usual suspects"— Tricia Suellentrop, Amy Alessio, and Patricia Taylor— for their time, energy, and ideas. And always, thanks to Erica for her support.

I'm fifteen years old and I'm driving a stolen car.

Ashley, my best friend forever, sits beside me. Despite my long light-brown hair, I'm the Goldilocks of the interstate: not too slow, not too fast. The speed is just right to avoid attention, while taking us far away from Flint, from family, from friends, and from a summer filled with faithlessness.

I don't want a stolen car; what I need is a time machine to reverse the past two months of my life. Before all this, if someone was doing a word association game and said my name—Danielle Griffin—the word "normal" would have been the right answer. Since I kept my home life hidden from most, I was just another under-the-radar sophomore at Carmen High School. I used to read books and think, "Why couldn't something exciting happen to me?" But I'd trade all the turmoil of the past two months in a second to have my boring loveless life back.

And it is love, or something like it, that has us heading

north on I-75 through the hot and muggy August Michigan air. I'm not sure how any of this will end, but for now, I'm driving a stolen car on a steamy starless night, wishing I could vanish into the black void.

JUNE

1

FRIDAY, JUNE 13

"Can't you just shut up?" Carl yells at Mom, then slaps her across the face. The smack of flesh on flesh echoes over the booming rap music from a passing car and the rumble of an airplane flying overhead. These angry sounds aren't new, just freshly delivered this Friday evening.

Mom stands there, stunned for a moment. She's probably wondering—I can only assume, since Mom and I are not really on any serious speaking terms—what to do and who is this person she's allowed to invade our lives. "Bastard," she hisses, then heads back to the kitchen.

Carl, the latest Dad wannabe, is inhaling his food in front of the TV. He asked Mom to get him yet another beer. Unlike Carl, she's worked all day. She's only home for a few hours from her Laundromat job before heading off to night waitress at the Capitol Coney Island. She told him to get off his lazy fat ass and get it himself, not that Mom is one to talk about fat asses, nor am I. If it hadn't been about the beer, it would have been about something else—even if it was really about nothing. They're always one spark away from the next explosion.

He'd been sitting—the way he has for most of the past nine months—with his fat farting behind on the big brown sofa in the living room. That sofa, along with my mother's bed and the bathroom, is where Carl spends the greater part of his day. He watches TV, drinks beer, takes money from Mom's purse, plays softball, and mostly stays out of my boring life. Mom must have really pissed him off—also nothing new—to get him off that sofa. He bolted from his TV viewing spot to the dining room table in record time, slapping Mom's heavily made-up trying-not-to-look-thirty-one face. Her look is hurt, not surprised, which leads me to believe that while I'm seeing this for the first time, it probably isn't Carl's first strike. In the past nine years, other wannabes have left their marks on Mom's face, my back-side, and both of our lives.

"Get out of my house!" Mom shouts as she stomps back in the room.

"Shut up!" Carl slurs, then retreats to his sweet spot on the sofa. He's not much different from Stan, Mitch, or the rest of the men since my real dad left us back when I was six. Just because these men talk themselves into Mom's bed doesn't mean they can get into my life. Mom says these men love her, usually just before they leave her.

"I said get the hell out of my house!" Mom shouts back at Carl, then walks from the small dining room into the even smaller kitchen. Carl's fat face below his balding skull is red-hot with anger, while my mother's face is so tight that the brown roots of her dyed blond hair stand out even more than usual. The blood dripping from her nose sprinkles her face with red specks.

"Get your own beer!" Mom yells as she stomps back into the living room and hurls a white plate in Carl's direction. The plate lands with a thud near the still-blaring TV.

"Go ahead, break them all!" Carl shouts as he balances himself to stand.

"Fine!" Mom bellows, then heads back into the kitchen. As Carl follows her, he pushes his finger hard into my shoulder and then points toward my room, like he's trying to protect me from all of this. But Carl's not a protector or a provider; he's just another poor choice. Before I can move, or he can say anything more, another plate flies toward him. He deflects it with his arm, and the sound of it crashing mixes with the rumble of thunder outside to rattle every window.

"Fine yourself!" Carl shouts back. He grabs one of the half-filled bowls—pasta and sauce from a jar—off the table and throws it at Mom. It misses, crashing on the floor, sending shards of porcelain all over the kitchen. With the red sauce splattered on the dirty white tile, it looks like a serial killer's grisly crime scene, lacking only the police tape.

None of this seems real, yet it's all too familiar, like something from a TV show or teen problem novel. That's why I only read fat fantasy novels: I need to escape for hours into a different world from the one I'm living in. In my life, the dragons are my dark thoughts of doubt, loneliness, and fear. If this were a magical kingdom instead of a trailer park, then some knight or wizard would come to the rescue. But rusting cars, not shining armor, fill the pitted streets of Circle Pines, so it's up to me. I need to be my mom's heroine, just like those brave hearts I read about in books. I will be Danielle the Defender. I bolt from the table as they continue hurling dishes and insults at each other, and run into my bedroom to grab my cell to dial 911. The cell is the only luxury in my life, even if it is a piece of crap. By the time I push the last button, it sounds like someone is throwing glasses—or maybe beer bottles—onto the floor.

I suck it up, tell the 911 dispatcher what's happening, and give them our address. The address is almost unnecessary; the prefab metal trailers at Circle Pines attract Flint cops like a magnet. I bury my face in a pillow and scream until my throat becomes as raw as my life. As the sound of yelling and smashing rages on in the other room, I pray for silence to get me through this summer. I spent last school year taking tests and answering questions. I studied math, French, English, history, and science, but never learned what I wanted most to understand. Thinking about Mom and all the Carls in her life, then remembering Reid—the only real love of my life—I know there's only one thing I need to discover. I want to find out if love is real.

· · ·

"You won't even miss me, will you?" I mumble as I escape before the police arrive. I throw on my army jacket, making sure my cell and Camel cigarettes (stolen from Carl) are in one pocket and a Tamora Pierce fantasy is in the other, then head out into a light rain. I need a vacation, not from school—summer vacation started yesterday—but from myself, starting tonight.

I grab my bike from the small storage shed and pedal my pudgy legs like pistons down the flat backstreets of Circle Pines. There's a crack of thunder and a harder rain starts to fall. I bike up Maple Road, over the bridge at I-75, then let the wet wind blow back my hair as I coast downhill toward the 7-Eleven at the intersection. It seems like I've spent so much of my life riding uphill. As I let gravity pull me faster, I wonder when I'll get to coast through life, instead of always pedaling so hard.

At the 7-Eleven, I pull my bike under the awning, catch my breath, and try not to think about the scene I've just left. The test comes tomorrow: if the locks to the trailer are changed, then I'll know Carl's yet another failed Dad wannabe. If not, then he's getting another chance. I wouldn't miss anything about Carl other than the cigarettes I lift from his coat during his post-softball six-pack-inspired naps. I light up a Camel and blow thoughts of its previous owner away.

I lean against the wall and think about calling my BFF Ashley, but hesitate. What I really don't need now is Ashley's predictable, compassionate, yet unrealistic advice. I need to laugh, so I try Evan. Evan's my best boy friend but not my boyfriend, much to his disappointment. I just don't like him in that way, no matter how hard I try. Evan's nice, sweet, maybe even a little cute, but he's my sidekick, not my love interest. Still, at times like now when I'm feeling down, I know that he'll make me feel good about myself. He's the anti-Carl—though I suppose that at one time, Carl made Mom laugh too.

"Is Evan there?" I ask the male voice who answers the phone.

"One second," he responds. After a cough, I hear him shout Evan's name. A few seconds of silence, another cough, and he comes back on the line. "No dice, sweetie."

"Do you know when he'll be home?" I ask.

"Whenever, I guess," is his less than helpful answer.

"Just tell him Danielle called," I say, ready to click him.

"Oh, his girlfriend."

"I'm not his girlfriend," I announce, then pause as the male voice on the other end launches into another laugh-induced coughing fit.

"Maybe you're just his big squeeze, huh?" the voice asks.

"Whatever." Maybe I'm overly sensitive, but I cringe at the word "big." My growth spurt was after eighth grade, when my baby fat went into my breasts and butt. I don't try to act sexy, but my eighth-grade wardrobe no longer fits my eleventh-grade body. Evan's interest—and other boys'— seems in direct relationship to my increasing cleavage and cup size.

"Evan says you're his girlfriend," the voice says. He sounds bored; I'm his entertainment.

"Who is this?" I ask in order to change this sore subject.

"I'm Evan's older brother, Vic," the voice says. The two things I know about Vic are that Evan doesn't like to talk about him, and back in the day, he used to hang around Reid's house.

"Tell him I'll call him back," I say. I won't let Evan call me at home; it's my rule so my mom doesn't find out about this boy who likes me. Mom has a rule that I'm not allowed to go out on dates until I'm sixteen. Mom has a rule that I can't be over at any of my friends' houses unless an adult is home. Mom has a rule that I can't have friends over unless she's home. Mom's rules are better suited to a toddler than a teen, and all of them show she doesn't trust me. Like most of my clothes, those rules don't fit me anymore.

"Evan's working at the mall," Vic says. "If you need a ride, we could roll."

"No, thank you," I say. I've heard enough of Mom's boyfriends high to detect the buzz in Vic's voice. I don't feel much like being alive right now, but I've got no interest in dying.

"Fine with me," Vic answers, then I end the call. I push number one to speed-dial Ashley.

"Hey, Danny," Ashley answers. She sounds out of breath too, but I know it's not from smoking: she's straight-edge and substance-free. With the schedule her parents have her on, even in the summer, I don't know when Ashley will get a chance to breathe, relax, or even play her most important role as my best friend forever.

"This is last minute, but could I come over and spend the night?" I ask, true to form. I know I ask far more from Ashley than I give her in return. I didn't need to get a B+ in algebra last year to know that our friendship's an unbalanced equation.

"Let me tell the 'rents," Ashley says, meaning her parents.

"Thanks," I say, knowing I'll have to summon a second round of courage to ask them to make the drive to get me—Ashley lives about five miles away. But her parents seem to like me okay, and I like being at a clean, sober, and shout-free house whenever I can.

As I wait for the answer, I will it to be a yes. There's no place else in this big world to go. My grandmother lives in Florida, but she and Mom haven't talked for years. The only other option is my mom's older sister Abigail and her family—including my soon-to-be-married twenty-four-year-old cousin Brittney—but they live about two hundred miles north up in Traverse City. Aunt Abby's husband is a doctor, but even he can't stitch together our fractured family. No wonder Ashley means so much to me: without her, I wouldn't have any lightness in my life, just loneliness. I'd be Danielle the Dark Warrior.

"The 'rents say it's a go," Ashley says, but adds, "But can you have your mom drive you over? The 'rents say they are in for the evening."

"Shit," I mutter under my breath. Ashley's parents are nine-to-five types with General Motors. They don't keep the same odd and ever-changing low-wage hours as Mom. Still, eight o'clock on a Friday night seems early to be in for the evening. They're also old, a lot older, I guess, than my mom. Maybe almost forty-five. Ashley doesn't talk much about her parents other than normal complaints, so I respect that. There are certainly things about my miserable life I've never shared with Ashley, either. I notice the rain has mostly let up, so I say, "I'll bike over."

I wonder what will happen next in my house. Carl might go, but probably not to jail. The police are probably there now, but Mom won't press charges. Instead, she'll change from mad to sad and Carl will be back in our house and her bed. There's a formula for it: the number of beer cans will decrease and the talk of "attending church" or "going to college" will increase. People always grumble about how stupid math is, but it helps me understand life. Like Carl and all Mom's boyfriends before: they all have a common denominator. They're all common and they all bring her down. Life's a fraction: somebody's on top, somebody's on the bottom. I'm not sure how I got stuck on the wrong side of that line.

As I bike toward Ashley's, I think more about when I'll start driving come October. Driving always makes me think of my dad. One of the best memories I have is of him behind the wheel with me on his lap. He had this old Corvette convertible and every weekend in the summer, we'd go for long drives: top down, radio on. No matter which direction we went, whenever I was with my dad, it seemed the breeze was always behind us. Then when I was six, something happened between my parents, and he was gone. And lately, it just feels like Mom and I were born to run against the wind.

. . .

"You remembered it was game night, right?" Ashley asks in a whisper the second I walk in the door.

"Welcome, Danielle," Ashley's mother says as she walks into the room. She's always polite.

"Hey," I mumble in return. Her natural grace makes her seem to tower over us even though she's shorter than both Ashley and me. I kick off my pink Chucks so I don't trample my Circle Pines filth into her always immaculately clean house.

"Let me get some iced tea for you both," Ashley's mother says, exiting as smoothly as she entered.

"Make hot chocolate instead," Ashley says as we make our way downstairs to the basement. While I'm trapped in one little room in our cramped, crappy trailer, Ashley's got a big bedroom, and this huge finished basement where we usually hang out.

"Are we still going shopping tomorrow?" I ask nicely. The politeness of Ashley's house sticks even to me.

"She wants to come with," Ashley says, pointing upstairs. "When I told her no, she suggested that I could just give you some of her old clothes, like you'd want to wear them."

"Your mom dresses so nice," I say. Ashley's mom dresses for success; my mom's biker-chick chic. "Just like you do, Ash."

"You can't wear any of my clothes!" she says. Ashley's taller than me, but weighs less. She's almost five eight, but not much more than a hundred twenty pounds. She's not all freaky bony like some of the model wannabes at school; she's just tall and thin, which is weird, since both her parents are short and round. But I know her thinness is natural, not some Lifetime-movie eating disorder. No way could my best friend keep a secret like that from me; besides, I've seen her eat more than me, but never gain a pound. She's born lucky, I guess. She's got long brown hair that sometimes falls in front of her big brown eyes like a mask, dark thick eyebrows, never-needs-makeup skin, and full lips. Ashley's beautiful.

"Is everybody decent before I descend?" Ashley's father yells from the top of the stairs.

"He's so weird," Ashley whispers to me and I nod in agreement.

"I'm walking down the stairs now," he says. "One, two, three."

"Forget it," Ashley cuts him off in her most disgusted voice. "What do you want?"

"Just inquiring when you'll be emerging," he asks, then almost runs back up the stairs.

"Just tell me when the hot chocolate is done, okay?" Ashley shouts up the stairs, then sighs.

"How can you be cold when it's summer?" I ask.

"I'm always cold," she replies, then points into the laundry room. "Sometimes I just want to jump into the dryer."

"What do you mean?"

"It would be like being back in the womb—warm, safe, and surrounded."

"I guess," I say, then laugh. Ashley's full of crazy ideas.

As we wait for her parents to summon us, we sit in the basement talking about our summer plans. Ashley has lots, although most have been designed by her parents, like her weekly piano lessons. I have no plans other than to avoid my house as much as possible. Both of us will go to a book club at the Flint Public Library. We met at the Carmen school library, where I worked at the start of our freshman year. She was looking for a book, while I was looking for new friends. Most of the Circle Pines crew were making the transition from junior-high binge drinkers to serious high-school stoners. My main junior-high friend Kate and I blew up the year before, so the stars were aligned when I met Ashley that first week.

I hear the door open at the top of the stairs; the sound coincides with an Ashley sigh. Ashley can sigh and roll her eyes better than any parent. She uses those moves at school for the most stupid teachers, but reserves the best for home, in particular whenever her mom talks.

"Hot chocolate's ready!" Ashley's mom exclaims. I can't picture Ashley's mom yelling; I can't imagine a day in my house where my mom doesn't scream at me.

"Can you bring it down? We're comfy," Ashley says, throwing a blanket over our feet.

"Let me know when you girls are ready to come upstairs," Ashley's mom says as she hands us the drinks.

Ashley just rolls her eyes, then mouths the words "game night." At my house, it's fight night. Maybe boredom is the price you pay for peace.

"They're nice people, but so dull," Ashley says, then rolls her eyes again.

"You're so lucky."

"And you're so wrong," she snaps back.

"I just wish you could walk a week in my Chucks with Mom, Carl, and their bullshit," I say, trying to hold back tears. Truth is, Ashley wouldn't last a day in my shoes; she'd sprint home and hug her mother so tight she'd probably suffocate her. "It's getting so bad."

"What's wrong?" Ashley asks, and I finally tell her. I've hinted to Ashley before about some of the stuff going on at home but never told her much. Like kids with their MySpace accounts, I've been living two lives: the one most people see at school as this normal boring kid and the other at home with the shouting, drinking, and now hitting. Telling Ashley everything feels like I'm infecting her. I'm Danielle the Disease Carrier. As I start telling her about Carl hitting my mom, I'm thinking to myself about why I'd called 911. A year or so ago when Mitch lived with us, I never thought of calling the police when he slapped Mom. I didn't get smarter, braver, or even wiser in the past year, I'm just getting angrier: at Mom, at the Dad wannabes, and mostly at myself. I used to be afraid of what might happen. Now I'm just mad.

By the time I finish recounting the events of the evening,

I'm in tears. I think Ashley wants to sob too, but can't or won't. After two years of friendship, I've yet to see her cry. Instead, she'll just stare off with this faraway look in her eyes, almost as if she's in a trance. Her jaw gets tight and her wide, innocent brown eyes look so much older.

"You did the right thing," she says after I finally calm down. "You love your mom, right?"

"Of course I do," I reply. Ashley knows no matter what I say, that's how I really feel.

"You tell her that?"

"Probably not enough," I admit.

Ashley sighs. "Well, you could tell her a million times, but what matters is showing her."

"Showing her?"

"Like tonight, you protected her," she says. "That's what love is really all about."

"How did you get so wise?" I ask Ashley, only half joking. Ashley likes to talk in absolutes and clichés, like she's a wizard in a fantasy book. But I don't think Ashley's ever been in love, and I've never confessed to her about when I was thirteen and fell in love with Reid.

I start looking through her DVDs. I need to get pulled into a fantasy world and away from these long-hidden thoughts of Reid. I haven't loved anybody since him. Sure, I've kissed other boys at dances and all that stupid high-school stuff, but they only pretended to like me. I'm sure they like two things about me, and they aren't my heart and my soul.

Ashley chooses a movie about another hero on a quest, but the treasure I seek this summer is different. I'm trying to discover how you can fall in love when you've failed in the past and you don't have any people in your life to show you what love really looks like.

2

SATURDAY, JUNE 14

"It's her best book ever, don't you think?" Ashley asks me in front of the book club at the library. She's pointing the new Tamora Pierce book at my yawning face like a sword. We'd stayed up late last night watching DVDs. Truth is, I can't help but think about fighting my everyday dragons rather than mythical fire-breathing beasts in books and movies.

"I guess," I mumble through the cookie in my mouth. As others voice their opinion, I feel embarrassed, not just for trying to talk with my mouth full, but for not backing up Ashley. When we first started book club, I barely spoke unless Ashley or Mrs. Acevedo asked me a question. I wasn't like them; I hadn't read every book in the world. Ashley's life is as simple as mine's complicated. She goes to school and gets good if not great grades; she goes home, reads, and does stuff with her parents. She goes to ballet, piano, and other classes, and one day she'll go to a good college, marry a fine man, and have a great life. She gets her kicks by escaping into imaginary empires, but to me, her perfect house and family already seem like a fantasy.

As Ashley and the others talk about the book, it's hard for me to focus. What good is talking about a magical kingdom ruled by strong women when my mom's getting slapped in the face? I start to wonder about the other kids in the club and the secret lives they lead. Like Lauren, this gorgeous girl from Central. She's got perfect skin, short blond hair, and beautiful blue eyes. She comes to book club with two friends, both beautiful as well, although Lauren's the fairest of them all. They're best friends, so they have a code between them. I tried hanging with them last summer, when Ashley went on a mid-July vacation with her parents to New York City, but I didn't click. It was like I was in a band with them, but always a beat off. Next to their brains and beauty, I felt like a slow and ugly stepsister, especially when they all talked on and on about their cool boyfriends.

Lauren always reminds me of Reid's sister, Kate. Kate and I were BFFs in junior high, but that seems so long ago. I couldn't be friends with her now, but not just because of Reid. It's because she's everything I'm not. She's stylish, tanned, and perfectly proportioned; I'm pale, clumsy, and lumpy. Her makeup is always right and her clothes look painted on, while no matter how I try, I always look sloppy. But it's more than her looks; it's her confidence. Kate knows she's always going to get the guy; I know I'm not. That's a lesson I learned from her in eighth grade. Because she's confident, she almost glows; because I'm not, boys must smell the sweat of my desperation. Mom gets mad when I say things aren't fair. I should remind her of Kate, and that'd shut her up.

"Hey, Danny, we gotta catch the bus," I hear Ashley say, tapping me on my shoulder. I'd totally tuned out the discussion. I promise myself next time I'll read the book.

I briefly rejoin the conversation, which involves how we're all going to get together outside of book club, but we never do. Ashley and I say our goodbyes, then head to wait for the bus to the mall. I'm thinking about visiting Evan, who works there and invited me to lunch.

By Halloween, I won't be on my bike or buses like this any longer. Once I can drive, my life is going to be so different and so much better than it is now. It won't be like all those mornings last year when Mom and I would pull into school in her lame, rusted Malibu, while a bunch of seniors roared past us laughing even louder than the music pouring out of their Escalade. Somehow, I'll get myself in that other car, the cool car; I won't be trapped in that Malibu anymore.

• • •

"You want some fries?" Evan asks, dangling the tempting salt stick in front of me.

"No, thanks," I reply softly, like I don't want to be heard over the low roar of the mall's food court. I'm hungry, but hate eating in front of any boy.

"Thanks for stopping by. It's nice to have a chance to ketchup," he says as he dips one of his fries into a small white container of Heinz. I roll my eyes, although nowhere near as dramatically as Ashley, as Evan punishes me with puns. "I relish this chance to see you."

"Whatever."

"Lettuce talk about it." Evan's trying to keep a straight face. "I'm in a pickle to find a bathroom because I must—"

"I talked to your brother," I announce to end Evan's unfunny pun fest.

Evan wipes the sweat from his brow. Like me, Evan's carrying more pounds than he should. Add that to the heavy red Halo Burger uniform he wears while working over a hot grill, and it's no wonder he's sweating. "That's a bad idea," he says. I wait for a smirk or smart-ass remark, but instead he just fiddles with the ugly hat that covers his cute curly brown hair.

"What's Vic's story?" I ask.

"It's a short story," he says. "He's Poe; he ain't got no money. He's a real Dumas."

"Serious up, Evan." I should also add "eyes up," since Evan's eyes tend to drift down.

"My brother Vic is a loser," Evan says, then sighs. He bites into his burger. I try to ignore the speck of mustard clinging to his top lip.

"What does that mean?" I ask.

"He moved back home because he got evicted from another apartment," Evan says. He sounds embarrassed; he's blushing almost as much as the first time he asked me out. He also sounds sad, almost as sad as when I said no to that first request, and all subsequent ones. "Vic's your typical stoner story: dropped out of school, got into some trouble with the law, out of work most of the time. He smokes weed and plays video games. He's useless, but you're lucky."

"Lucky?"

"To not have brothers or sisters," Evan says as he pushes his half-eaten burger aside.

"What do you mean?"

"It's a lot of pressure having a brother like Vic," Evan replies, his smirk long gone. "Since he's messed up his life, my parents are on me all the time to do better in school, to work harder. If Vic wanted to ruin his life, that's fine, but he didn't need to wreck mine as well."

I pick up a napkin off Evan's tray and wipe the mustard from his lip.

"Sorry to be such a downer," Evan says. "Vic will do that. He'll just bring you down."

"Okay," I say, then snatch a fry off Evan's tray.

"Why are you talking to my brother anyway?" Evan asks, then cracks another smile. "Are you trying to learn what I'm really like? What I look like naked? Because I could—"

"No, thanks!" I can't decide to laugh, smile, or gag at the thought of Evan naked. Mostly I wonder if he's thought of me that way. "I called you last night and he answered the phone."

"Vic lives in our basement," Evan says, then grunts. "He's more mushroom than man."

"He doesn't sound so bad," I say.

"What do you mean?" he mumbles while sipping soda through a straw.

I try not to let Evan see my smile as I say, "He sounds like a real fungi."

Evan spits soda out of his mouth, then starts laughing. He looks cuter when he laughs. He's not bad-looking, but he's not totally hot, either. Truth is, he's a lot like me.

"There's one good thing about having him around, though," Evan adds.

"What's that?" I ask, bracing myself for another joke.

"He's like a role model on how not to live my life." Evan gets all serious again. "I can ask myself every day about everything Vic would do, then do the opposite."

I don't say anything. I smile to cover for the brooding dark thoughts already overtaking me about my house, my mom, my life, and my choices. We sit silent for a while until Evan announces he's got to get back to flipping Halo Burgers.

As I get up to leave, he leans over to kiss me. I turn my mouth away and he makes a wet spot on my cheek. I feel closer to him after this conversation, but I still don't want him to kiss me. I guess I should be happy that he likes me, but as I watch him walk back to work, I fall back into my brooding, knowing that for Evan—and Evan alone—I am Danielle the Desirable.

· · ·

"So how was Evan?" Ashley asks as I meet her outside the food court. She's spent the time shopping for books. My limited allowance barely covers library fines, let alone new novels.

"Boring, as usual," I say, not sure why I need to put Evan

down, especially in front of Ashley. Ashley's not a big Evan fan. She never says anything ugly about him, but she's not very encouraging, either. I think Evan has mutual feelings of disinterested jealousy about Ashley.

"You ready to go get bathing-suited up?" Ashley asks.

"I guess," I say, then take a deep breath. In about a month, Ashley will be coming with Mom and me and maybe Carl to my cousin Brittney's wedding in Traverse City.

"So this hotel has a nice pool?" Ashley asks.

"I think so. There's also a beach on Lake Michigan we can go to."

"I've never been to a beach," Ashley says.

"Never?" I reply. I'm flashing back to more memories of Dad. We'd often end our Corvette trips at one of the small beaches around one of Michigan's many lakes, although the drive was as much fun as the actual destination.

"Do my 'rents look like people who go to the beach?" Ashley asks, then sighs. "They barely leave the house on nights or weekends. Maybe they're reverse vampires."

"No, my mom is a vampire," I say. "You know why?"

Ashley starts to answer, but I beat her to the punch line.

"Because she's sucking all the fun out of my life."

"We'll change that. We'll have lots of fun in the sun!" Ashley says, pulling a wad of cash out of her expensive pre-torn jeans. Her parents definitely leave the house long enough to go to the bank, as Ashley's never without money to spend. She's told me she's got enough to buy us both nice bathing suits, as opposed to the Kmart crap that my mom gave me money for.

"Thanks for doing this with me," I say. Like Ashley's mom, my mom wanted to come with us, but the days of Mom picking out my clothes are long gone. Her taste in clothes is as bad as her taste in men.

"I bet Evan would help you shop for a bathing suit," Ashley says as we head toward Aeropostale.

"He'd rather help me shop for my birthday suit," I remind her.

"Too true," she says, then laughs.

Like most kids at school, Ashley dresses like everyone else and looks like no one in particular. If you fit in, then you don't stand out: nobody notices normal. Trendy clothing stores scare me. I see those mannequins and freak out at how the world thinks I'm supposed to look.

We shop for over an hour and Ashley keeps window-shopping at every store. She drags me into some, but mostly I just hang out while she tries on different outfits. I don't like to shop, since I don't have any money to buy anything. It's like going to a restaurant, staring at the menu, but not being able to order. It just makes me hungrier, but even hungry eyes are better than going home.

At Sears, Ashley suggests a few suits, but I don't like any of them. Finally, I find a solid black one-piece, over which I'll probably wear a too-big T-shirt to cover my too-big body parts.

"Are you sure?" Ashley asks, arching a skeptical eyebrow.

"Sure," I say as she hands me cash to pay, then we leave the store and sit down on a bench. Like a mind reader, she can tell something's wrong. She leans toward me, and I take the bait.

"Last summer, Mitch took us to the beach and I don't think I've ever been more embarrassed. Mom was rolling around in the sand with Mitch half the time, which was bad enough, but when she wasn't, she was parading around in her two-piece red bikini."

"So!" Ashley's never been to the Circle Pines pool or a beach with Mom. If she had been, she'd know.

"My mom's legs, arms, and even her back are all tattooed, mostly roses and crosses."

"Really!" Ashley says, showing interest rather than the disgust I feel.

"Ash, you know how you always say you're embarrassed by how your parents act!" I ask. She nods, then sighs. "Well, for me, it's not what my mom does, it's more just who she is."

"I bet she doesn't embarrass you in public like the 'rents do," Ashley says.

"All the time. When Carl and Mom aren't arguing, they're all about kissing in public."

"Big mistake," Ashley says. "How grotesque!"

I nod my head; I'm opposed to any public display of affection. But what I proclaim to be hate is really jealousy. What I hate most are the things I want but don't have. It's like there's a party I can see through the window, but I can't find the door to get inside.

"Thank God the 'rents don't kiss in front of other people!" she adds.

"Evan just tried to kiss me in public," I tell her, half-embarrassed and half-flattered.

"Not cool," Ashley says. "No offense, but your puppy is kind of pathetic."

"Evan? Why do you say that?"

"I mean he's so in love with you. It's almost embarrassing to be around," she says. "Thank God you're not like that about him, or anybody."

I bite my bottom lip to have an excuse for my oncoming tears. "What's wrong?" she asks.

"Nothing," I say, as my eyes dart to the right.

"It's good you play Uno and not poker."

"What do you mean?"

"You're lying," she says. "You can lie to your mom, but you can't lie to your friends."

"I *was* like that once, before we met." I start to confess a secret I should've told a long time ago.

"I thought I knew everything about you." That Ashley's never heard the story proves I'm so boring that all have forgotten my eighth-grade embarrassment. "So tell me now!"

"Really, it's nothing," I say, wishing I could just shut up for once.

"If it's nothing, then you *can* tell me," Ashley says, then arches her eyebrow again. "But if it is something, you *must* tell me. Best friends tell each other everything, always."

"Okay, but let's get out of here in case you get mad," I reply as I rise from the bench.

She stands close beside me, then asks, "Why would I get mad at you, Danny?"

"Because of who I loved and why I loved him," I start. "It's pretty shameful."

"I promise I won't get mad, but I need to know." She sounds excited. "Who was it?"

"My best friend's brother," I say as we walk down the hall and I slide into my past.

. . .

"So, how about some details?" Ashley asks as she sucks on a milk shake.

We're back in the food court. We find a table near the back, far from Halo Burger in case Evan's still working. Even though the place is full of screaming babies, cell phone conversations, and teens shouting at nothing, it seems like Ashley and I are alone in the world.

"You know Kate Barker?" I ask. She nods.

"Kate and I were best friends," I say. "Then in eighth grade, we both liked the same boy: Sean Simpson. He was so cute. Only boy in eighth grade who didn't act like a junior-high jerk."

"I think I'm going to barf," Ashley says, then sticks out her tongue at me. Sean's in the same grade as Ashley and me but not in any of our classes. He probably spends more time in detention than he does in class. My guess is next year he won't make it through eleventh grade.

"It was kind of awkward that we both liked him, being best friends and all."

"Don't worry, I have no designs on Evan," Ashley jokes.

"Now *I'm* going to barf!" I say, then stick my tongue out and point my fingers down my throat.

After she's done laughing, she says, "So, you, Kate, and Sean in a big love pie."

"No, Kate and Sean as a couple, me sitting alone," I reply. It's been years, but the memory still itches like a partially healed scab.

"Poor Danny," she says, slightly sarcastic, mostly sympathetic.

"I can't tell you how much that hurt," I say, trying not to lose it in public. "It wasn't just my best friend doing that to me, but it made me feel so bad about myself. Kate's prettier than me, and cooler than me. I realized then that no one would ever want me or love me."

"Why didn't you tell me any of this?" Ashley says, sounding a little hurt herself. "BFFs are not supposed to have any secrets. It's part of the code."

"This isn't just a secret," I say. "This is something to be ashamed of."

"Sometimes they're the same," Ashley says, looking away from me. It sounds like she's got something more to say, but she stops herself, then turns back to me. "What happened?"

"It hurt so bad. I went from adoring Sean to hating him," I say, accenting my words with a loud sucking sound. My milk shake's gone; my anger isn't. Not at Kate, or Sean, but Life the Unfair.

"You should have been mad at Kate."

"Oh, I was. I decided to get back at her by flirting with her older brother, Reid. I'd known him growing up. After the thing with Sean, I started thinking about him *that* way."

"How much older?"

I try not to look her in the eyes. "I was almost thirteen; he was eighteen."

"How grotesque!" What makes Ashley a great friend is her predictability.

"So I started spending more time at Kate's house, not just because I wanted to stay away from my house, but because I wanted to see Reid. I thought I'd flirt with him, not that I really knew how. If I could get his attention, I thought that would make Kate mad. Then somehow we'd be even. You do a lot of stupid stuff in junior high."

"I guess," Ashley mumbles.

"I found myself thinking about Reid all the time," I say, trying not to smile. "He had this look, this side-of-the-mouth smile, that said, 'I don't care what anybody else thinks.'"

"I know the type," Ashley says. An odd remark, but I let it pass.

"Even though I wasn't supposed to be hanging out at people's houses if their parents weren't home, I started hanging out over at Kate's place after school. I tried to plan my visits for when I thought Reid and his friends would be there. One of them, I think, was Evan's brother Vic, but I'm not sure since Reid was the only person I cared about. So, one night I was over and they offered us wine coolers. I swear, Ash, it's the only time I've been drunk."

"Nobody's perfect."

"Eighth grade seems so long ago, and all of this sounds so stupid now, but then, all this drama mattered so much." I really hate myself for starting this conversation. Although I've given Ashley endless details about my regretful make-out sessions with immature and uncool boys over the past two years, I've hidden this story because it hurt so much, which means it was real.

"So?"

"I guess I had too much to drink. The party was winding down and people were going off into corners to make out. Kate and Sean started making out and I just felt desperately alone."

"Loneliness and liquor, a bad team," Ashley says, trying to make me laugh.

"There were all these girls hanging on Reid, but none acted like his girlfriend, so I . . ."

When I pause, Ashley prompts me, "So I?"

"He was on the back porch having a cigarette. It seemed like my only chance. I told him how cool and cute I thought he was. How much I liked him. How much I'd thought about him."

"So did the two of you—"

"He just stared at me, then he laughed. At first, I thought it was nervousness, but he was laughing at me like I was some stupid kid. Which I was. I got flustered and went back inside."

"And what happened?"

"He told his sister that I'd come on to him," I say. "I remember

Kate yelling at me. I thought it would make us even, and that would cause us to be friends again. But instead of us making up, she just said a bunch of mean stuff, and then she told all Reid's crew."

"So did you and Reid ever hook up?"

"I really don't want to talk about this anymore."

"Danny, if you can't tell me..."

"Remember, I was almost thirteen," I remind her, then sigh. "I ran out of the house. I remember calling my mom to pick me up, crying the entire time until she arrived. I was destroyed."

"Danny, I'm sorry," she says, putting her hand on my shoulder.

"Reid was my first real crush. It's stupid to say now, but I thought I loved him. But not only didn't he care, it seemed he didn't care if he hurt my feelings either."

"You must have been so embarrassed." Ashley states the obvious.

"I was for a while, but within a week, this other girl in our class found out she was pregnant, so everyone was on to the next scandal." I sigh again.

"So what happened with Reid?" Ashley asks.

"I was too humiliated and hurt to see him again, and Kate got so mean," I say, choking up at the memory. I'd taken one leap forward only to be slapped two steps back.

"He never apologized?" Ashley asks. "What a creep. So, where's lover boy now?"

"I don't really know. I don't talk to Kate anymore, and the

kind of people who hang around Reid are not people I want to hang around with." This is a lie. Reid and his pals were always the coolest kids in school. Kate told me once how Reid showed up at school on Monday wearing his belt backward, and by the end of the week, everyone was doing the same.

"Well, you have better friends now," Ashley says.

"Ash, you know what bothers me most?" I ask, but before she can answer, I say, "I remember all of this so well, but I just know Reid doesn't even remember me at all."

"That might be for the best."

I stand up, then say, "Let's get out of here. I need a cigarette."

We drop our trash, then head outside to the bus stop to soak up the warm sun, but now I feel cold. No wonder I never talk about Reid; it depresses me and leaves me feeling bitter.

We're silent for a while before Ashley asks, "Did you ever tell him off or get an apology?"

"No, I never talked to him again," I answer.

"That's sad," she mumbles.

"Do you think I should have told him off?" That question has plagued me for years.

"I don't know what you should have done, Danny, but I just know you need to make peace with your past," Ashley says, looking into the distance like she's beyond all this drama.

"What do you mean?"

"You can't have it hanging over you like a hammer," Ashley the Wise Wizard says as she stands up. No doubt, the bus is rounding the corner.

"I don't care. Why should I forgive him?"

"I don't know if you can forgive someone who's never said he's sorry," she says with that all-knowing look in her eyes. "You just need to make peace with your past."

"Whatever for?" I say. I pull the killing smoke deep into my lungs.

Ashley points at the bus headed toward us. "The past's a big stone; you can push and kick it as much as you want, but it's not moving."

"How did you get so smart?" I ask her, but her only response is a sigh. I put the cigarette out under my foot. "Where were you in eighth grade when I needed all this great advice?"

Ashley laughs but doesn't answer as we climb on the bus, finding a seat near the front. Almost immediately, she opens up a book. She's reading, I'm brooding again. Next to the bus is a metallic blue Shelby Mustang with the windows down, rap music blasting, and the people inside—two girls, two guys— laughing like their lives have never been unfair and they've never been happier. I've got to figure out a way to bridge the distance from my sad little trailer-park porch to the front seat that always seems so far out of my reach.

3

MONDAY, JUNE 16

"Why don't you ever trust me?" I yell at my mom. Inspired by my visit, Evan called six times yesterday and twice this morning. I've just hung up the phone in the face of Mom's fury. She's convinced these phone calls prove that I'm breaking her no-dating rule.

"In October, when you're sixteen, you can date," she says, putting out her cigarette in her coffee cup. It's her signal that the conversation is over. "You just have to wait a few months."

"That's not fair," I shout at her.

"Do your parents let you date?" Mom asks Ashley. I try to avoid fighting with Mom in front of Ashley, but sometimes she drives me so crazy that I can't control myself. I can barely hear over the loud sound of Carl's snoring from Mom's bed. He rejoined us for church yesterday morning and hasn't left the house since. That means Mom smoothed things over with the police and Carl's getting yet another chance. But if he's staying, then I'll need to find more excuses to stay away from the trailer this summer.

"This isn't about Ashley, this is about me," I say. I think Ashley's parents *would* let her date, if she wanted to, but I can't risk it. Besides, Ashley looks more upset than me, probably because conversations in her house rarely are loud enough to be overheard by neighbors.

"I don't see why you want to screw up your life, Danielle," Mom says sharply.

"How is one date going to screw up my life?"

"You really don't understand boys, do you?" Mom says, breaking out her smug I-know-so-much-more-than-you-know look. "Maybe when you do, then we can talk about this."

"Like she's going to teach me," I tell Ashley, but loud enough for Mom to hear.

"What does that mean?" Mom asks. She knows, of course.

"What do you think it means?" I counter. A little voice inside is telling me to shut up, but facing a whole summer's worth of Carl makes my words fall like hard driving rain.

"We're done!" Mom gets up from the dining room table and heads toward the kitchen.

I shout after her, "Why don't we ask Mitch, Carl, or—"

"I said enough," she hisses back at me.

"Or Eddie, Vince, or whoever else you've dragged into this house."

"Another word and you're grounded!" She stares me down. I stare back. I won't blink first.

"Or we could just ask Dad, if we knew where he was," I shoot back. Inside I smile; a few days' grounding is worth it to bring all this out into the great wide open. I turn away from Mom to share my victory with Ashley, but all I can see is the back of her head.

"Ashley, I'm sorry!" I shout after her as she runs out the door.

"You don't listen. You don't learn, Danielle, that's your problem," Mom says.

I'm torn: wanting to stand and fight with my mother; wanting to run and help my best friend; wanting to grab Carl's truck keys off the table and drive away, not that I know how to drive. I take a deep breath, not to calm down, but to fire up. "Just because you messed up your life, don't assume I'll ruin mine." I say it so fast I don't know if Mom hears me. She doesn't respond right away.

We just stare at each other in the cool of the morning, no doubt both feeling that same hot blood pumping through our veins. Mom finally speaks. "Go check on your friend, Danielle."

I unclench my fists, break my stare, and head out the front door.

Ashley's sitting on the three-step porch in front of our trailer. A plane rumbles overhead, while bass from a car somewhere booms. There's never space for quiet reflection at Circle Pines.

"You okay?" I ask when it looks like she's ready to talk.

Ashley sighs, then says, "You shouldn't talk to your mother that way."

"What?"

"Look, I don't want to fight with you too, but you *can't* do that," she says. If her words had weight, the word "can't" would have weighed a ton.

"Just because your parents are—"

"This isn't about the 'rents," Ashley cuts me off, then stares at the butts of smoked cigarettes littering the area around our tiny porch. "Your mom is your mom, always. No matter what you do, no matter what you say, no matter what happens. Your mom is always your mom."

I start to speak, but Ashley interrupts me again.

"If you don't believe that, you don't believe in anything," she says. She puts her hand on my knee, gets up, and starts walking barefoot across the concrete, away from our trailer. I hurry back inside, gather up her stuff—including her shoes— and a few things for myself, and make sure to avoid my mother. That's easy to do; she's in the bathroom, probably wishing the shower water could wash away all her troubles. I take one last longing look at the keys to Carl's truck and run to catch up with Ashley.

"You wanna walk over to Wal-Mart?" I ask. Ashley is sitting in the grass in front of a sign welcoming people to Circle Pines. Truth is, someone should warn them to stay away.

"If you want," she says, brushing the grass from her jeans.

"I just don't want to be here," I say, reaching out a hand to help her up.

"I thought you were grounded."

"Big deal," I say, feeling the urge to spit. It wasn't like I had many places other than Ashley's to go anyway. "It won't stick."

"Why do you say that?" she asks as we start walking north up Torey Road.

I stare at the hard road in front of us, then tell her, "Because she knows I'm right."

. . .

After killing a couple hours walking around Wal-Mart, mostly making fun of all the stupid stuff that people buy, we cross Hill Road to eat at McDonald's. Ashley pays, since I'm cash poor as usual. In the middle of eating, her phone rings. It's her Mom tone.

"I know, I know," Ashley says in a singsong voice, then hangs up. "I gotta go. Piano lessons today."

"Sounds like fun," I say, but I can only guess. Ashley's so spoiled it stinks.

"Piano lessons are *not* fun!" She taps her fingers loudly on the table.

"Must be nice to have parents who buy you stuff."

"The 'rents do come through," she says, trying not to smile.

"I guess when your parents love you, then—"

Ashley's smile abandons her as she says, "Never confuse love and money."

Her mom picks us up from McDonald's during her lunch hour, then drives us home. Without actually saying the words, she makes it clear that I can't hang out with Ashley at her piano lesson, and that after the lesson, Ashley has plans that don't involve me. Her parents like me, but I don't think they like that I live in Circle Pines. I thank her for the ride, say goodbye to

Ashley, then decide to walk to Evan's house, which is pretty close. I try to call, but he's not answering and my batteries are near death. After Ashley's mom's car is out of sight, I light up a cigarette and walk slowly toward Evan's house. With all this hardness in my life, why shouldn't I settle for his sloppy soft kisses?

"Is anybody home?" I yell, banging hard on the door of Evan's house. I'm just about to leave when I hear the garage door opening. There's a loud sound, like a car without a muffler, and a billow of white smoke. I cough once, then walk over to the garage.

"Is Evan home?" I shout over the racket. A guy's in there working on a rusty old gold Grand Am. The hood's popped up, so all I can see is a pair of beat-up old white Converse sneakers.

"Who wants to know?" he asks, then the hood closes. The guy's sporting a worn black Pink Floyd T-shirt, which matches his short black hair. He's got two silver rings in his left eyebrow, a small star tattoo on his neck, and a scruff of beard. He looks very familiar.

"I'm his friend Danielle," I say as I start to back away slowly.

"We talked on the phone," the guy says. He wipes his hands on a rag, then holds out his right hand, which I shake, trying not to give off any hint of recognition. "I'm Vic."

I try not to look him in the eye. He doesn't seem to remember me from Reid's house.

"He's working today," Vic says.

"Okay," I cry over the noise.

"Hey, sorry I can't turn this junker off—I'm not sure if it would start again!"

"Okay," I say, wondering why my years of reading books with advanced vocabulary now leave me able to speak only one word.

"I need to get this piece of shit out on the road. You wanna ride to the mall?" he shouts.

"No, that's okay," I tell him, taking one step back.

He takes two steps forward, then says, "Look, you're my brother's girlfriend and—"

"I'm not his girlfriend," I remind him. I'm guessing he's only being nice to me to help his brother's endless if futile quest to label me his lady fair.

"Well, he thinks you are, and that's what matters," he says, then walks away from me. Once he gets near the passenger door, he shouts, "I'm not going to hit on you, I'm just offering you a free ride. You can stand here in this killer sun or you can get in. Your choice."

He doesn't seem drunk or high. He's not really a stranger, and I think he's telling me the truth. Since I'd rather be any place other than home, I take a little risk. "Okay."

"Cool," he says, leaving the car door open. I climb in. The car smells of smoke, and Vic lights up a Newport almost as soon as he sits down, like a reflex. I take the cue and pull out a Camel, but he says, "Hey, you're too young to smoke."

"You sound like my mom," I crack, but he doesn't laugh or even grin.

"I'm serious," Vic says, and I put the cigarette back in the pack. "It starts with that, then you start smoking weed, and before you know it, you know what you become!"

"No, what?" I ask.

Over the rattle of his junker car, Vic mumbles, "Someone like me."

. . .

"So you know Evan from school?" Vic asks as we rumble down Fenton Road. I can tell Vic doesn't remember me from when I hung out at Reid's. Either he's smoked too much weed or I'm just not that memorable.

"Yeah, from school," I say. It's hard to hear him over the engine and the heavy metal music he's turned on that's shaking the car's already creaky frame.

"He's good in school, not like me," Vic says, tossing his spent cigarette butt out the window. The car hasn't got any air-conditioning. My window's broken and only rolls down halfway. I feel myself starting to sweat, from heat and from nerves.

I'm not sure what to say. Does he want me to reassure him? Ask him a question? I'm better with adults than with people my own age, but clueless about in-betweens like Vic. He looks older, maybe twenty, but he lives at home. He's not a child, not a teen, but certainly not an adult.

"He's probably going to go to college," Vic offers. "How about you?"

"Probably," I mumble. Mom always says I'll go to college, but I have no idea.

"I wish I'd stayed in school and gone to college, but maybe someday I'll go," Vic says. "I gotta get out of Flint, maybe drive down south or go up to Canada."

I'm speechless as I realize that Vic reminds me of Mom. Same crappy car. Same regret list. Same hope that a good-luck lightning bolt will strike. Same dreams that turn into lies.

"I got to get another job and a better set of wheels," he adds.

"What do you do?" I ask. Since so few of Mom's boyfriends actually have or keep jobs, I'm curious about what Vic thinks he can do.

"I install car stereos," he answers. "I hate working for other people, so I got fired by my asshole boss at Best Buy. I'll find something, maybe."

"Good luck."

"Maybe Evan can get me a job at Halo. As hard as he works, he'll probably manage the damn place before he's out of high school." He laughs. "Little bro is all right."

"He's a good friend," I shout, making sure that anything I say that might get back to Evan won't get misrepresented and give him any false hopes of making me his "big squeeze."

Vic doesn't say anything. Since we don't have much in common, I just let the music fill the void. Vic's right: Evan's a good kid. All last year, he'd talk with me at school, always gently asking me out, even though I always said no. Evan tries so hard, and that's the problem. You shouldn't have to make someone like you. I know Evan will be there for me, but I can't tell Vic that his little brother is always going to be my plan B.

"Hey, I gotta make a stop," Vic says casually. "It won't take too long."

"We're still going to the mall, right?" I ask.

"Hell yes," Vic says.

"I need to call my mom. My battery's about dead. Do you have a cell?"

"Go ahead," he says. He reaches into his pocket and hands me what would have been a super-fancy cell phone four years ago. Now it's another junker, like his crappy car.

There's no answer at home, but before I can leave a message, I'm distracted. I hadn't been paying attention, but the neighborhood we pull into off Jennings Road is familiar. Too familiar. Before I have a chance to say anything, we're parked in the driveway of Kate and Reid Barker's house.

Vic gets out of the car, then waves at me. "Hey, move over to the driver's side."

"I don't know how to drive," I tell him.

"If you hear the car start to stall, just pump the gas," he says. Before I can tell him I don't even want to do that, he's gone into the house. I move myself over to the driver's seat and sit clutching the wheel, my right foot filling with a thousand sparks. My dad used to let me pretend to steer, but other than arcade games, I'd never really sat behind the wheel before. I feel my hands shake, but then I realize it's just the car starting to stall. I pump the gas, hear the roar, and smile. I turn the rearview mirror so I can see myself. Staring into the mirror, I imagine myself behind the wheel of my own car, my friends in the car with me, music playing, and everybody laughing as we tear down the highway.

I turn down the face-melting metal Vic put on. With the volume lower, I can now hear the sound of a booming bass coming from inside Kate's house. In between songs, I hear lots of shouting. Not angry shouting like my mom and Carl do, but shouting to be heard in the middle of a party. In the middle of the day. While Mom doesn't throw parties, there are few weekend nights in Circle Pines when someone isn't hosting one. Most of the time they're loud parties, with lots of empty beer cans on the street and at least one visit by the police. I usually sit in my room, headphones on and eyes in a book, trying to ignore the sounds—not because they aggravate me, but because deep inside me, I feel them call me like sirens.

I'm lost in my thoughts with my eyes closed when a tapping sound startles me. I open my eyes to see, through the cracked and dirty windshield, Reid Barker's bright green eyes and brighter smile shining like a crescent moon.

• • •

"Danielle, right?" he says as he slips around to the driver's side of the car.

I run my fingers through my messy hair, smile back at him, and say, "You remember?"

"Of course I remember you," he says as he touches the small gold ring embedded in his left eyebrow. His arms are tanned and tattooed; there's a dark green fire-breathing dragon at the top of his right arm. He's shirtless, so there's a lot of skin, and not an inch of fat, to see.

"Is Kate home?" I ask, hoping he won't catch the mix of sadness and relief in my voice that he didn't greet me by saying, "Oh, Danielle Griffin, I remember you. You're the girl who got drunk, came on to me, got rejected and humiliated, and then disappeared."

"She's spending the summer with Dad over in Port Huron," Reid says. He's kneeling by the side of the car, leaning in to talk to me. "It's just me and Mommy Dearest here."

"I don't see Kate much at school anymore," I mumble. Truth is, I don't want to see her, and she doesn't want to see me, so we avoid each other.

"Well, let's get a look at you," he says. He backs away from the car, then opens the door. He's wearing worn black pants with a big gold belt buckle to match the gold rings and studs in his eyebrow and ears. He's got a light-brown soul patch on his chin and he's wearing a backward black cap that pushes his hair back onto his shoulders. He's still gorgeous.

"Vic said I needed to sit here and make sure the car doesn't stall," I say.

"Vic's an idiot," he cracks. "I'll take care of him if he messes with you."

"Okay, I guess." I run another quick hand through my hair.

"The stories I could tell about Vic are—" He stops short when I stumble in my usual clumsy fashion getting out of the car. I'm just about to fall fat facefirst onto the driveway when

Reid reaches his arms out to save me. I end up with a slightly scraped elbow.

"Thanks," I mumble, my face turning scarlet as it points toward the gray concrete.

"Good Goddamn, woman!" he shouts as I stand up. "You look fine!"

My eyes stay frozen on the ground. I realize the last time Reid saw me was probably in eighth grade before I grew into this body. There's a lot more for him to see, so I instinctively move my arms to cover my eye-magnet breasts. I'd started the day thinking I'd just be hanging with Ashley, so I didn't put on much makeup and dressed in my usual ill-fitting—in this case one-size-too-small—black T-shirt and pair of scuffed-up jeans. Reid must be lying: God hasn't been good to me. I don't look fine or like a woman. I just look like me.

"Hey, you're bleeding," he says softly, and touches my left elbow with his right hand. I notice that he has numerous small circle-shaped scars on the top of the hand, as well as on his arms.

"I'm all right," I answer quickly.

"You better take care of that," he says. "Maybe Vic can kiss it and make it better."

"Vic's not kissing me," I tell him.

"Like I said, Vic's an idiot," he says, and I blush.

"I'm friends with Vic's brother."

"Didn't know the Victim had a brother," Reid says. "Maybe if Kate comes home this summer, she can hook up with him instead of the loser she's been hanging around with."

"Evan's really nice," I say.

"So, he's your boyfriend, good for him," Reid says, but I just shake my head and frown.

"Really? Well, hey, you should come inside, we're just chillin'," he says, pointing toward the house. The music and shouting don't seem as loud as they were before Reid came outside.

I look back down at the ground to avoid his green eyes sucking me in.

"Well, we gotta fix that cut," he says, touching my elbow again, then showing me the blood on the tip of his finger. He points to a big scar on his left arm. "This is what happens when you don't get stuff taken care of."

"Skateboard injury?" I say, remembering that Reid and his pals were hardcore skaters.

"Skating sucks," he says, making me feel stupid. "No, it comes courtesy of the same thing as the rest."

Reid takes my right hand, then grabs my index finger and runs it softly across the scars on his left arm, ending with a large one just below the shoulder. "Old gifts from my asshole father. He used my skin as an ashtray. I fucking hate that flesh-burning bastard."

"Oh my God, Reid," I say, pulling my hand away and then covering my mouth.

"Is your dad an asshole too?" he asks.

"My mom's like that," I say, yet even as the words exit, I know they're not true. I don't hate Mom; I just hate some of the things she does and says. As bad as things are, she's never done anything as horrible to me as what Reid just told me his dad did to him.

"Wow, I don't know why I just told you that," Reid says, leaning closer.

"I won't tell anybody," I almost whisper.

"Our secret then," he whispers back. It looks like he wants to say something else, but he gets distracted by some guy on the porch yelling his name.

"You sure you don't need me to fix that?" Reid asks.

"I'm fine, I'll fix it at home," I reply, so unsure what Reid really wants. What I want.

"I gotta get back inside. We're playing this cool new racing video game I just scored. It's my turn to get behind the wheel, kick some ass, take some names, and make them bow to the master!"

I nod and turn to get back into the car, which luckily hasn't stalled.

"God, what a piece of shit Vic drives," Reid says, opening the car door for me. "Maybe one day he'll have a kick-ass car like mine."

"Which one is yours?" I ask, looking at the cars and SUVs that fill the driveway.

"Check out that cold-as-hell Viper," Reid says as he points to a flaming red sports car with fancy silver rims. Before I can respond, Reid lays a small tender kiss on my cheek and says, "Great to see you again, Danielle. Any time you wanna come back over, it's cool."

"Thanks, Reid," I say, stumbling over my words as I sit in the unfamiliar driver's seat.

"I'll tell Vic to get his head out of his ass and get you wherever it is you want to go," Reid says. I'm back in the car, but my hand is on the door, underneath Reid's scarred paw. He gives my hand a gentle squeeze, then puts his fingers to his lips, kisses them, and touches the cut on my elbow. I'm embarrassed and overwhelmed, so I avert my eyes.

"Hey, look at me," he says, reaching his hand into the car. "You got a cell?" I answer by handing my phone to him. He turns it on, then quickly punches in a few numbers—his, I pray. He doesn't say anything after that. He just walks away, which causes my head and heart to start spinning like an out-of-control merry-go-round. Seeing Reid again leaves me with both strange and familiar feelings, but it also creates one more question I need to answer this summer: is there any truth in the cliché that time heals all wounds?

4

TUESDAY, JUNE 17

"**What do you want to** do now?" Evan yells from the driver's seat of his mom's car.

"Let's just go someplace," Ashley says. She's not a fan of driving around in circles, but it seems right to me because my mind's been racing in circles ever since I saw Reid again.

"No, let's just drive," I say.

Evan speeds up, but he's still going way under the legal limit. "You want to go to the drive-in? Maybe to a drive-thru? Maybe we could do a drive-by? Go to—"

"Could we just get out of this car, please?" Ashley asks. It looks like she's carsick.

"Then where to, Ashley?" I turn to ask her. Sitting next to me in the back, she shrugs, then looks, almost trance-like, out the window. I knew she'd prefer it if just the two of us spent time hanging out, but Evan invited me to a movie, and I dragged her along so it wouldn't be a non-Mom approved date, much to Ashley's, and Evan's, disappointment. No matter what

I do, it seems that I just can't make anyone happy anymore, especially myself.

"Wanna get something to eat?" Evan asks.

"I don't have any more money," I confess. Evan probably would have paid for the movie if I hadn't brought Ashley with me.

"I have a Capitol idea!" Evan shouts. "Is your mom working?"

"I don't know," I say, stalling. When I got up this morning, she and Carl were already yelling at each other, so I left without saying goodbye. Their promises to change stuck like a cheap Band-Aid. "I don't care what we do or where we go, as long as I don't have to go home."

"I'm Hungary. I need Turkey but without too much Greece," Evan says, still trying to get a laugh.

"Can you just take me home?" Ashley sighs.

I take a quick glance at our location, a quick reading of the other faces in the car, and a deeper look at what I've been thinking about for the past twenty-four hours, and then say, "Why don't we see if Kate Barker is home?"

"Kate?" Ashley and Evan say in surprise at the same time.

"She lives near here, just off Jennings Road," I say, ignoring their reactions.

"I thought that you two were—," Ashley starts.

"I feel bad about what happened with us," I say, feeling worse about telling so many lies.

"If that's what you want, then just tell me where to go," Evan says.

"We don't have to stay long," I say.

"I need to be home in an hour. I have a ballet class," Ashley announces.

The loud music streaming out of the Barker house is anything but ballet background noise. There are a couple of cars in the driveway, most of them nicer than Vic's junker or Evan's Mom-mobile. Some older kids are sitting on the porch smoking. I don't know these people, but I recognize a few faces of seniors from last year and a few from Circle Pines.

"I don't know about this place," Ashley says to me as Evan parks on the street.

"Come on, Ashley, be cool," Evan says, although his voice sounds anything but.

I get out of the car and walk toward the house. The street's littered with cigarette butts, pop cans, and various fast-food trash items. I turn around to see Ashley still sitting in the car. Evan's outside at least, but he's not moving any closer.

I start to knock on the door when one of the longhairs on the porch giggles. "Kid, the door's always open at Reid's." The other guys laugh louder, then I go inside. The music hits first, the smell of smoke hits next, and the smell of pot hits last. All the shades are pulled, so even in the middle of a bright June day, it's as dark as December.

"Who are you?" some buzzed guy asks as he bumps into me. Like the guys out front, he looks a lot older than me.

"Is Reid here?" I shout over the music.

"He's in the cave," the guy mumbles, never even looking at me.

"The cave?" I ask.

"The basement, bitch. Get a fucking clue," he says sharply, then stumbles past me.

I stand there for a second, my feet feeling as heavy as stones. I think about Ashley and Evan, probably still in or near the car, then I think about Reid. I flick my tongue over my bottom lip, take a deep breath, and walk back out into the fresh air. I tell myself, "You can do this."

"Kate's not here," I tell Ashley and Evan. Ashley has now come out of the car. She's clearly uncomfortable with the scruffy-looking guys on the porch leering at her.

"Then let's get out of here," she says.

"No, let's just hang out here for a while," I say, all casual.

"Are you serious?" Ashley says, her lips immediately forming a pout.

"Let's meet some new people, that's all I'm saying." I smile. "Maybe we'll recruit some new book club members."

"They look like real honor-society types," Ashley grumbles, nodding at the two chimneys on the front porch. Then she points at Reid's car, surrounded by people in the driveway. "I'm sure *that* would make a great bookmobile."

"That's not just any car," I correct her. "That, Ashley, is a cold-as-hell Dodge Viper."

She rolls her eyes like dice.

"Don't worry, we'll get you to ballet in time," I say extranicely, trying to hide my frustration, not just because I want to see Reid, but because Ashley never wants to meet new people. I think she would be happiest if her whole world was her parents, her books, and me.

Ashley crosses her arms and frowns, so I play my trump card. "Do this for me. You know why I don't want to go home."

"Fine," she says.

Evan—in his khakis and white shirt—and Ashley—in her pink Hollister T-shirt and pre-torn jeans—look out of place among the dirty denim and long white T-shirt-wearing crowd. We walk back up the driveway, but Ashley and Evan make it no farther than the porch. The two smokers have vacated their seats, which Ashley and Evan immediately fill. "Just an hour," Ashley reminds me.

I nod, then head inside the house. I inch my way near the basement door, but hesitate. After a few minutes two big-haired, gum-smacking girls emerge. The door's opening creates an impromptu battle of the bands: the rap on the main floor colliding with the heavy metal from "the cave." I cover my ears, then walk downstairs, more unsure with each step. I tell myself again, "You can do this."

There's a big-screen plasma TV that takes up nearly an entire wall. Two guys wearing black ball caps are playing one of those Nintendo Wii racing games, while two blond-haired girls sit on a fire-red sofa. The girls are passing a beer between them, and shouting both insults and encouragement to the guys in their pretend race. The basement's filled with cardboard boxes and the smell of stale smoke, spilled beer, and sweat from the racer wannabes.

"Do you know where Reid is?" I ask the prettier one of the girls. Even if she tells me, I'm not sure I can take another step as the dual dragons of fear and doubt drag me down.

She snaps her gum like a gunshot. "Who wants to know?"

The other girl giggles, then whispers something to the prettier girl, who laughs louder.

"Is he here?" I ask again, trying to ignore them. I can tell they can't wait until I leave so they can laugh at me even louder. I know girls like this at school: they have this *look*, like they think they're better than you for no real reason. It's more arrogance than confidence.

"I know you," one of the girls says, then sips the beer.

"You work in the library at school," the other one says, then takes her small sip. They're dressed alike: tight black beaters, cut-off jeans, and sandals. One's a real blonde, one's dyed. Both are sporting too much makeup, perfume, and attitude. The only fashion difference between them is that the real blonde has a gold stud in her nose, while the fake blonde has a silver one in her eyebrow.

"I'm Danielle," I say politely.

"Let's call her the bookworm," the fake blonde cracks. "No, wait, just Worm."

"Oh, snap," the real blonde adds, then laughs so hard she almost spits up her beer. "Hey Worm, why are you looking for Reid?"

"Is he here?"

"You want some beer, Worm?" Real asks, offering me the bottle. I'm glad it's so dark down here, lit only by the flashing lights of the video game. That way they can't see how red my face is growing.

"She's not cool," Fake says in a tone of unmistakable cruelty as I hesitate for a moment.

"Thanks," I reply as I fight to control my shaking hand and grab the Budweiser. One beer just to show them I'm cool, but not enough to get drunk and humiliate myself in front of Reid yet again.

"Wait, I bet the Worm would prefer tequila," Real says as she pulls the bottle back.

"It's a mistake to waste good booze on little children," Fake says.

"Never mind," I mumble, thinking how this—and my life—is all one big mistake.

"So Worm's gonna slither away!" Fake shouts, then laughs, a drunk's loud laugh. I start up the stairs, trying not to fall and embarrass myself even more.

"What the fuck is going on!" I hear Reid's voice say from the top of the stairs.

I don't say anything. I just point at Real and Fake. Reid acts as if he understands me.

"Danielle, don't worry about their shit," he says softly, almost whispering in my ear.

"I don't belong here," I confess.

He puts his arm around me, pulling me toward him. "Hey, you're always welcome, unlike some people."

"What do you mean?" I ask, but he releases me with a kiss on the cheek, then heads full-throttle downstairs. I follow two steps behind him, then stay put at the bottom of the stairs.

"You and you," Reid says, pointing at the blond twins. "Get the hell out of here."

"What!" Fake says, her blue-caked eyes shooting daggers my way.

When they don't move, Reid walks over to the game console and unplugs it. "Dude, what's going on!" one of the gamers says to Reid.

"All of you, get out!" Reid's voice roars like a lion over the crashing music.

"Reid, man, come on, relax," one of the guys says, offering up his hand, but Reid slaps it away. The two blond girls remain frozen on the sofa. Fake guzzles down the remaining beer.

"Tony, Nick, get out. And take these skanks with you," Reid says, staring them down.

The two guys run upstairs in an instant, leaving the blondes behind. They move from the sofa and start stumbling toward the stairs, but Reid blocks their way. "Apologize first," he says.

"We didn't—," Fake starts.

"I said apologize." Reid cuts her off, pointing at Real.

"Reid, I'm sorry," Real says.

"Not to me, to Danielle," he replies. I've been standing by the foot of the stairs, but I take this as my cue to come closer.

"We were just kidding around," Real says to Reid in a flirtatious voice. She pushes back her blond hair and leans in to put her brown-lipstick-covered mouth next to his ear.

"Now." Reid shuts her down.

"Hey, we're sorry," Fake says. "Right, Angie!"

"Right. Sorry," Real adds. I take a step toward them, but Reid pulls me next to him. He quickly locks two fingers of his left hand around one of my belt loops. Angie seems like she wants to cry as they walk past us. Reid stares at them while pulling me closer to him.

"Reid, let me make it up to you," Angie says softly, but loud enough for me to hear.

"Get out," Reid says, then points to the top of the stairs. After Real and Fake are long gone, Reid whispers, "You okay?"

I shake my head. My brain and heart are firing like pistons in a hundred directions.

"Some people who hang here," he says, "well, they're kinda immature."

"It's okay," I mutter.

"They just come to play with my toys," he says, flashing that crescent-moon smile that reminds me why I loved him back in eighth grade. "I have the best toys."

I nod. Words can only get in the way.

"You ever play Race Car Hero?" he asks.

My yes nod turns into a no shake. If I don't say anything, then I won't blow this again.

"This game is cold as hell," he shouts, then walks over to plug the console back in. He hands me one of the players, straps it on, explains the game, and then turns on the action. He quickly sees that I'm not that good, having poor coordination, no driving skills, and even less video game experience. After we play for about twenty minutes, I'm exhausted, from concentrating, from laughing, maybe even from smiling too much in one day.

"You'll learn," Reid says as he unstraps the player from my wrist. "You just need a good teacher."

"Okay," I mumble. I can feel the rough texture of his fingers over my softer skin; I can almost trace the nerve impulses down my arm to my heart. He takes my hand, leads me over to sit on the sofa, and then gently pulls me toward him.

"Reid, I—" But he stops my words by putting his fingers on my lips.

"Danielle, when did you get so hot?" Reid whispers before he kisses me on the lips. His eyes aren't seeing some stupid junior-high kid. His lips aren't touching the lips of some immature girl. When I came over to the house, I didn't know what I'd do. Now, as Reid pulls me closer, I'm not sure what I'll do next—other than just about anything he wants.

"Danielle, are you down there?" I hear Ashley's voice yell from the top of the stairs. "We have to go!"

I remove my mouth from Reid's, but before I can answer, Reid whispers into my ear, "Who is that?"

"My friend Ashley; she came with me."

"She cool?"

Ashley is many things, including my BFF. But cool, as Reid defines and represents it, she's not. I don't want to lie, so I don't answer.

"You'd probably better go," he says softly, then plants a small kiss on my forehead.

"Okay," I say, as I run my hand through my make-out-messy hair. I used to be a silly eighth grader he'd rejected, but now I was a hot girl he'd defended when others made fun of me.

"If you ever want, you can come hang out with me," Reid says in parting. I head toward the stairs, then make my way out toward the porch.

"Evan's in the car," Ashley spits out the second she sees me.

"What happened?" I ask.

"You mean other than you ditching us?" Ashley replies. She's almost running toward the front door. With her long legs, it's a struggle to keep up. As I pass through the house, I see more faces I recognize from school, but they're mostly people I don't really know. There's maybe a dozen people inside—Fake, Real, and their boyfriends no longer among them—and another four standing on the porch. Everybody's laughing, or at least smiling. The weather outside is early-summer sizzling, but the temperature inside is as cool as can be.

"Look, Ash, I'm sorry," I say when we finally reach the sidewalk. She's standing, arms crossed in impatience and eyes flashing with anger.

She stares back at me, then heads to Evan's car. The Beatles song "Helter Skelter" is turned up full-blast when I climb in the backseat. Ashley puts herself next to Evan in the front.

"Why did you get in the car?" I ask Evan, but he says nothing. I sit in the backseat, arms over my chest and eyes pointed at the floor. Evan peels out, as well as a person can in a Mom car.

"Evan, please turn down the music," I finally say once we've pulled onto Ashley's street. Evan lowers the volume and I say, "Look, I'm sorry about what happened over there."

"We tried to call," Evan says. I thought it was odd how he'd used the word "we," like he and Ashley were a couple, which has been my goal for some time. I figure if he and Ashley hook up, then everybody will be happy, but they refuse to cooperate.

"My cell's dead," I lie. Truth is, I traded time without my phone instead of a grounding for making that Dad comment yesterday. My cell's doing thirty days locked in Mom's trunk.

"Where did you go?" Evan finally asks.

Ashley shuts off the AC, then turns to face me. I hesitate before answering, which gives her time to fill in what she thinks she knows. "She was in the basement getting high."

"I was not, I was just playing Race Car Hero," I mumble.

"I thought I was your hero," Evan jokes, and I crack a smile. I guess when you really like someone, you can't stay mad at them.

"Always, Evan, every day," I joke back, then gently kick his seat. He laughs and hands Ashley her Beatles CD as we pull into her driveway.

When the car comes to a stop, I quickly exit. I wait for Ashley to say something or shoot me a cross look, but instead she gets out and starts toward her front door. I circle around to the driver's side and motion for Evan to roll down the window.

"What?" he asks. I lean over, which is sure to distract him from any lingering anger toward me.

"I'm sorry," I repeat, then return his wet cheek kiss from the other day. He tries to turn his lips toward my mouth, but I hold him in place.

"It's cool," he says, not that Evan really understands what the word "cool" means.

Ashley waits for me by the front door. We both wave good-bye to Evan, then go inside. "Quick, into my room," Ashley says the second we cross the threshold.

She runs up the stairs, taking them two at a time. I get her bedroom door shut behind me just as I hear footsteps coming toward us. Seconds later, there's a light tapping on the door.

"Ashley, you're late. We need to leave in five minutes," her mother announces.

Ashley performs a little ballet move for my benefit, which cracks me up.

"I'll get dressed before we go," she says. "I'll hurry. I just need more time."

"Okay, fifteen minutes," her mother replies, then walks away from the door.

"We don't want to keep her waiting." Ashley finishes her sentence with a plié and eye roll. Her walls are covered with pictures of ballerinas, except for a large poster of John Lennon with the word "Imagine" that hangs over her bed. "Like you kept us waiting, Danny."

"Sorry, but I was—" I start to talk, but then cut myself off. It's too soon to tell her about Reid.

"Well, thanks to your little visit, we stink!"

"What!" I answer, still trying to catch my breath from the stair chase.

"We smell like smoke: legal and illegal," Ashley says.

"Do you have some perfume or lotion?" I ask, opening up one of her dresser drawers.

"Hey, how about a little privacy, friend!"

"Sorry," I mutter.

"You're just a sorry machine today," Ashley says. I think I see a smile peek through.

"Sorry," I repeat, all flustered, causing us both to laugh.

"I just don't want the 'rents thinking I'm smoking or getting high."

"But you didn't, right?"

Ashley finds a perfume she likes, uses it, then hands it to me. "No and never."

"Sorry for asking," I say, spraying the perfume. It gives me a reason to put my hand over my face, embarrassed for saying sorry again and embarrassed for thinking otherwise. Ashley doesn't like that I smoke cigarettes, and hates when I do it in front of her. At school, she's part of the Red Ribbon anti-drug club, which I joined with her as an act of friendship. For some people, Red Ribbon is just another club; for Ashley, it seems more like a crusade.

"What was going on down there?" she asks as she gets her ballet bag from her closet.

"What do you mean?"

"Who were all those people?"

I shrug my shoulders. I know one thing for sure: not only are the people at Reid's not book club members, they're not Red Ribbon types, either. No doubt, they all prefer the green leaf.

"I don't want to go back there," Ashley says.

"But it was fun."

"For you," she snaps back.

"Well, maybe you would have liked it if you hadn't just hung on the porch."

"It was the only place to hang and not have somebody pass you a joint," Ashley replies.

"Not everybody was like that," I say. Reid didn't seem stoned or drunk, but I couldn't tell her that or even mention his name, at least not yet. Like Ashley said, a little privacy, please.

"I don't like people like that," she says. It sounds like she's grinding her teeth.

"It wouldn't kill you," I tell her.

"What won't kill me?" she asks, still glaring at me.

"To drink one beer or smoke one joint," I respond.

"It only takes one," she says, adding, "Don't you know, Danielle? Drugs are dominoes."

"Officer Ashley, why are you so melodramatic?"

"And why are you so naive?"

"I don't use drugs," I remind her as I head toward the door.

"God, you don't get it, do you?" she says, almost blocking my way.

"What?"

"People don't use drugs, Danielle, drugs use them," she says.

"This isn't a Red Ribbon Club meeting, Ashley, so can you spare me the speech? Why do you talk about things you know nothing about?"

"Danielle, you don't even know what you're saying," Ashley says, sounding not so much angry at me as frustrated with herself. I don't answer. Instead I think about how she's going off to her perfect world of family-sponsored ballet lessons while I'm heading back to Circle Pines. We might be best friends forever, but we're not equals, not even close. She coasts through a lucky and luxurious life, while I've been pedaling uphill so hard for so long. But maybe, just maybe, Reid's gonna be my chance to bust out of Circle Pines for the summer.

5

FRIDAY, JUNE 20

"**Where's Carl?**" **I ask Mom,** who's sitting on the small three-step porch in the morning light.

"Gone," Mom answers. Her tone's an odd mix of sorrow and satisfaction.

"Good," I say, maybe too happily.

"Don't sound so pleased," Mom tells me. "You may not like him, and I don't ask you to treat him like a father, but Danielle, he is part of our family."

"Carl isn't my family," I reply. Ashley has a family; I have the wannabe parade, a long-gone father, and Mom. Carl tries to be nice, just like he tries looking for a job, but like his job search, he fails.

"Families are complicated, baby," Mom replies, then offers me her coffee, which I refuse. She doesn't offer a cigarette, however. She must suspect that I smoke, but she also knows she really can't say anything about it, given both her and Carl's two-pack-a-day habit.

I take the towel from my wet morning hair, so Mom can see my eyes when I repeat, "Carl isn't part of my family."

"He cares about us, that's enough," she says quickly, then takes a drag on her smoke.

"Whatever," I say.

I go back inside to get dressed, which will take longer than usual. I want to look good. I want Reid to see me again, just to prove that the other day wasn't a dream. Actually, I know it's not, since the past few days of not seeing him have left me sleepless.

"When you were in the shower, that Evan boy called again," Mom says when I emerge.

"Okay," I say, without much enthusiasm.

"You should be happier," Mom says as she motions for me to sit on the porch next to her. I need that cigarette now so we can have one of those Circle Pines mother-daughter moments.

"What do you mean?"

"Having some nice boy care about you like that," Mom says. Her voice is rough, and I realize it isn't the cigarettes or the years of secondhand smoke from waitressing. She sounds like I do, after I've been crying.

"So Carl isn't just not here, he's gone," I say.

"For now," she says, burning the tobacco down to the very last fiber. "I sent him packing again, at least for a while."

"Is he coming back?" I ask. Mom's looking off into the distance, over the concrete and the nonexistent pines of Circle Pines. As I wait for an answer, I study her for bruises. I heard yelling last night, but no more than normal—or so I thought.

"I don't know," she answers after a long pause, then puts the cigarette out under her ugly waitress-sensible shoe.

I don't say anything, but I feel another "sorry" creeping up my throat. I can't believe I have any apologies left to give. Truth is, I don't want my mom hurting, no matter what.

"Mom, can I ask you something?" I say, almost like I didn't want to be heard.

She pulls back her hair and rubs her eyes. I take that as a yes.

"Why do you let Carl stay after—"

"Baby, relationships are really complicated when you're my age," she cuts me off, then smiles. "I'm not eighteen or even twenty-eight anymore."

"But Carl is..."

"Look, Carl is Carl. He wasn't like this when I met him. Do you remember?" she asks, and I think we both flash back to last fall and how happy Mom was, and how nice Carl was to both of us. Mom's never happy when she's alone. "Well, I guess I'm just waiting."

"Waiting?"

"Waiting for him to be that way again," she says, trying to smile. "I know Carl's a good person inside or I wouldn't have liked him in the first place. The waiting is the hardest part."

I sigh in frustration, at Carl and at Mom.

"You just have to show a little faith in people, baby," Mom says.

"Why don't you start with me?" I say. "Why don't you trust me?"

Mom goes silent, then heads back into the house. Once

inside, she looks at me. And then she says, almost like it hurts, "I guess you should call Evan back."

"I will."

"He must really like you," Mom says, turning toward the kitchen. She quickly pours some water into a cup, stirs in some instant coffee, and puts it in the microwave. "I think it's kind of sweet, don't you?"

"I guess," I mumble.

"Boys are always going to like you, Danielle. You know that by now, right?" she says.

"I don't think so," I tell her, using Ashley's most sarcastic tone.

"It's just that you're so young."

"I'm not young. I'm almost sixteen," I remind her. "I'll be driving before I can date!"

"Danny, you're still my pretty baby, my special lady."

"Whatever, Mom, whatever." We both knew that "baby" was the magic word. It wasn't that I was her baby, but that she doesn't want me to have one. My mom's talk with me about sex when I got my period was short and to the point: don't even think about it.

"You'll have to trust me," Mom says.

"Trust you? You said I'm pretty. How can I believe anything you say?" I grumble.

"Let me show you something," Mom says, taking the coffee from the microwave. We walk toward her bedroom, and she actually lets me enter a normally off-limits area. She doesn't know, of course, that I look through her stuff all the time. She's rummaging through boxes in the closet, and I'm trying not to look guilty. I've learned more about my mom's life from snooping around her room than from anything she's ever told me. As usual, there are empty bags of chips and piles of magazines—*Glamour, Redbook, Cosmo*—on the floor, but not a single book. Most of the dresser drawers are half-open and her non-work clothes, mostly jeans and T-shirts, spill out.

"Danielle, look at this," Mom finally says, pulling a shoebox from the closet. She motions for me to sit down next to her on the floor.

"What is it?" I ask, wondering both what's in the box and why I'd never found it before. Maybe Mom's better at hiding things than I imagined.

"Promise not to laugh," she says, then laughs herself. A nervous laugh.

"Promise," I reply. She pretends to spit in her hand, as do I, then we shake. One of the Dad wannabes—I think Mitch—taught us the spit shake. It's gross, but it's cool too. And it's ours.

"Okay, this is me at your age," Mom says as she hands me a classic school picture. She was wearing a big black T-shirt and trying not to smile. Her hair was light brown and greasy, and her skin was pretty bad, even with all the makeup. She looked like a scared, self-hating fifteen-year-old. She looked like me. "I don't know why I didn't show you this before."

I bite my tongue. I want to say about a hundred things. For instance, "You never showed me because you never cared." But I figure there's something else going on here. I know my mom

better than she knows herself. If she's doing something nice—
and this *was* nice—she wants something in return. That's how
she succeeds as a waitress and survives as a single mom.

"Now, let me show you something else," she says, obviously
not wanting to look at the picture of her fifteen-year-old self
any longer than necessary. "This is me at sixteen."

I hold out my hand to take the picture, but she clings to it
for a few seconds. "What happened?" I ask, looking at this
slightly older version of my mom. Her skin had cleared up, she
was thinner and wearing a tight top, her hair was dyed blond
and done up—ridiculous but right for the time—and her smile
was sly, half-sexy and half-smirky. It's the same cool "I don't
give a crap" look that Reid wears.

"Things change," Mom says as she hugs me. "Never think of
yourself as not pretty."

I need a camera to capture this moment: my mom acknowledging my feelings, offering empathy, and reaching out to me.
"Thanks, Mom," I say, trying not to cry.

She takes the picture from me, returns it to the box, and
pulls back her hair. I lean into her, kind of, just soaking up the
moment. We sit together in silence for a while, then she finally
looks at her watch. "I've got to get ready for work."

"Okay, Mom," I say, and pull myself off the floor. I start
toward the door as she fumbles with the pile of makeup on one
of the dressers.

"I just want to protect you, baby. I know how men can be."

I shake my head. The parade of wannabes has taught me

that lesson just as well, although Mom seems intent on repeating the same course over and over again.

"I don't want you to make my mistakes," she adds, sipping some lukewarm coffee.

"You have to trust me."

"I do trust you, Danny," she says, then laughs. "But I don't trust teenage boys."

"They're not all like that." We both know I'm lying. She lets it pass.

"I just don't want you to—," she starts again, but I cut her off.

"To have a baby at sixteen, to make your same mistakes," I say.

"No, it's not just that," she says. "I don't want you to make the biggest mistake."

"What's that?"

"To think your life can't be complete without a man," she says, softly and sadly. "That's what I most want to protect you from, baby."

"Thanks, Mom." I don't know what else to say. For once, she isn't treating me like a child.

"But I guess you need to make your own mistakes, right?" she goes on. "Maybe I've been wrong in not letting you do that."

"It's okay."

"Just protect yourself, that's all I'm saying."

"You mean—"

"No, not just that," Mom says. "I know you kids know all about that stuff, not like us when we were growing up. I know you, Danielle. I know that you want a better life than this, a better life than me. I know you're too smart to do something so stupid, like I did."

I suck in every word of my mom building me up, even if she puts herself down to do it.

"No, I'm saying protect yourself from getting hurt, that's all." She sighs.

"I will," I promise her and myself.

"I can't shield you forever," Mom says. "It is just so hard to trust—"

I interrupt her. "What did you say, you have to show a little faith in people?"

She laughs, rubs my head like old times, then after a long pause says, "You should call Evan. And if he wants to take you on a date, then it's okay with me."

"So, it's okay if I have a real boyfriend?"

"Yeah, baby, it's okay," Mom says. Another sigh, another smile, and then we do the spit shake again.

I wipe my hands on my pants as Mom gulps down the rest of her coffee and gathers up her purse, cigarettes, and car keys on her way out the door. I don't think she's put the car in reverse yet before I start dialing. She hasn't even pulled away when I hear the word "hello" and say, "Reid, it's Danielle."

• • •

"So how's Kate?" I ask Reid, my head spinning, both from being with him and from just coming off what seemed like a hundred revolutions on the merry-go-round.

"All right, I guess. We don't talk much," he says as we move over to the swings at Fenton Lawn Elementary playground. Afraid Mom might return, I asked Reid not to pick me up at my house; instead, the Viper swooped me up at the 7-Eleven at the bottom of the hill. I left my bike behind.

"I should call her," I say quickly, trying to hide my nervousness.

"I'll get you her number," he says, but he doesn't reach for his cell phone.

"I feel bad about how things went down with her."

"Hey, shit happens," he says as he pulls out a cigarette. Then we're both silent, a big change from the ride over, which was filled with rap music blasting and Reid's cell ringing.

As he's lighting up his Newport, I say, "I'm sorry about what happened before."

He's quiet for a second, then says, "Well, I was just a kid."

"So was I."

"Well, you're not a kid anymore," he says, offering me the smoke. I take it, and he leaves his hand on my leg. It tastes nasty, but Reid's touch makes everything feel good.

"I guess not," I mumble, then hand him back the smoke.

"I mean it, Danielle, you're so grown-up." His fingers dance around my leg.

"Really?"

"I'm glad you're not still mad at me. You're pretty cool to hang with," Reid says.

"I liked you," I admit, realizing that "like" is the strongest emotion I'll confess to. Now.

"Your hair looks great. It's a lot longer now," he says, brushing it away from my face. "And I think your smile is bigger too."

I blush, the red in my cheeks almost strong enough to reflect off his white T-shirt. I stare at the ground below us, when his hand lands on my shoulder. He starts moving his thumb slowly and softly up and down my neck. The short hairs stand up tall.

"Hey, Danielle, look at me," Reid says. Then he whispers, "Let's go back to my house."

"Is your mom there?" I ask hesitantly as waves of guilt, doubt, and fear lap at my feet.

"If she's sober, she's at work. You never know." His smile vanishes as he takes a long drag on the smoke.

"I'm sorry," I say. "That must be rough."

His thumb runs from my shoulder down my arm, making small circles as he speaks. "I just try to stay out of her way. I live in my basement—the cave. I keep my door locked and my friends away when she's around. Our understanding is, we don't get into each other's business."

"You have a lot of friends."

"What can I say?" He winks. "I'm just a popular guy."

"It must be nice," I mumble, feeling jealous, seeking sympathy.

"Hey, you hang with me and you'll be fucking queen of the ball," he says, then laughs.

"Okay."

"Better than okay," he says, and he kisses me. The kiss is longer than before, harder at first and then softer. His tongue's teasing the roof of my mouth, while his hands explore my body, starting at the shoulder, then slowly working their way down the sides of the lowest-cut shirt I own.

He finally breaks the kiss, then whispers, "So you wanna come back to my house?"

"I don't know."

"I'll let you play with my toys," he says. "Like I told you, kid, I got some cool toys."

"I thought you said I wasn't a kid anymore," I say softly.

"You're all woman." He moves in for another kiss.

"This is pretty fast for me," I say truthfully. He frowns, but doesn't move away.

"Then your other boyfriends have been pretty weak," he says.

"Well, they were just stupid immature boys."

"You're better than that," he purrs. "You understand me, not like everybody else."

"Really?"

"To other people, I'm just a party guy," he says. "But I know you can see the real me."

"And you understand me too, I know." Now I'm thinking: so that means this thing between us is real. I wish I could tell him that what I want most is to be like him, with his great car, his always-ringing cell phone, his house full of friends, and his eyes full of confidence.

"You're so hot," he says. His lips aren't on mine anymore, but his hands continue to race around my body from knee to shoulder, and all the places in between.

"I just don't think of myself that way," I confess.

"Baby, then *that's* the only thing wrong with you," he says.

"Really?"

"Really."

I answer by kissing him. I lean against him and don't push his hands away. We move from the swings to the slide. I lie down, feeling the steel, hot from the summer sun, against my back. Reid's on top of me, sliding his tongue in my mouth and his hands under my shirt. I pull him closer, trying to remember how to breathe. I'm on fire: all the oxygen in my atmosphere is burning up. When his hand slips between my legs, I break away and scoot from underneath him to the ladder of the slide. He doesn't say anything for a second, then starts laughing loudly and climbs up the slide to the top. He takes off his shirt, pounds his chest like some alpha-male gorilla, and slides down. I rush to kiss him when he reaches the bottom.

"Your turn," he whispers. Does this mean I'm supposed to take off my shirt? I'm too embarrassed, not just about Reid seeing me, but about what might happen if some little kids come into the park. Still, I climb up and slide down, and he greets me with a kiss. I respond with wild laughter.

"What's so funny?" he asks.

"I just love that feeling of going down the slide," I tell him. "It's like how I love coasting down a big hill on my bike."

"You ever hit that big-ass water slide up in Frankenmuth?" he asks.

"No, I really don't..." Before I can finish, he's already shifted gears.

It all happens quickly. I use his phone to make sure Mom's at work, then slip into my house to get my bathing suit. I'm back in the car in thirty seconds and we're busting down the freeway at well over eighty mph, landing us in front of a water park in Frankenmuth, this tourist town north of Flint, in less than an hour. All the way up, Reid's talking really fast about the water park, then about us going skiing or snowboarding in the winter. As we're speeding down the highway, Reid's racing through the past few years, telling me about things he's done, stuff he's had, cars he's owned, and stunts he's pulled. I've been barely alive while he's been really living.

A sign says that the water park is for registered hotel guests only, but Reid starts talking to the girl running the ticket booth. I don't know what he says to her, but she laughs once, and then he waves for me to join him. He gives me a quick kiss, then we go into the locker rooms to change. He comes out wearing blue jean cutoffs, while I debut the black bathing suit, sort of—it's still hidden under a too-big T-shirt.

"Here comes my girl," Reid says, plenty loud enough for the tacky tourists to hear.

"What do you want to do?" I ask him, pointing at the sign listing the rides.

"Everything," he says, leaning in next to me. "But first I want to see you. All of you."

"Wow" is all he says when I peel off the T-shirt. He grabs my hand and pulls me toward the biggest slide. As we climb up, he's touching me the entire time. I should be feeling self-conscious about showing my body, but I'm not. Pretty soon, we're at the top of the sixty-foot waterslide. I get ready to slide down, but he wraps himself around me. We laugh all the way down, and hit the pool at the bottom with a mighty splash, earning dirty looks from everybody. We visit everything in the park a few times, like we owned the place. After about an hour, I'm exhausted from laughing, splashing, and climbing. I wish I had a camera so I could prove that all of this is real.

On the way home, Reid plugs his iPod in, turns the speakers all the way up, and rolls down the top of the Viper. We race south on I-75, going well over seventy-five miles an hour, but my heart's beating even faster. We circle my trailer once, making sure Mom's Malibu isn't parked out front. Reid leaves with a kiss good night, and I head off toward bed to sleep, but not to dream. What happened today was better than any dream I've ever had, and all I need to do tonight—and, I hope, tomorrow—is keep reliving it.

6

FRIDAY, JUNE 27

"Why do you want to go back over there?" Ashley asks.

"It'll be fun," I goad her. I've gone an entire week without Reid. The withdrawal's teaching me how addicts must feel. We've talked on the phone, but he's been too busy to see me.

"Those people were pretty scary."

"Give it a chance," I say. "Let's go over tonight." Although I can't admit it to Ashley, some of Reid's friends scare me too, but the reward's way bigger than any risk. Still, even if she and Evan don't come into the house with me, knowing they're around is important. Sometimes I think friends are like mirrors: you can't really see yourself without them looking back at you.

"Okay, maybe," Ashley says, without enthusiasm. We're sitting by the pool at the Ambrose house, which is a couple of doors down from Ashley's. They're away on vacation, and Ashley's parents arranged for her to dog sit. Banjo, Buster, and Pippin frolic in the large backyard, jumping in and out of the pool and amusing themselves with dog toys while we talk.

"I think there are a lot of cool people," I suggest.

"If by cool, you mean stoned," she replies.

"Not everybody there is like that," I tell her, still holding back Reid's name. I have to tell Ashley about Reid eventually but I hope I can keep him secret until I know for sure it's real this time.

"I'm just saying," Ashley says.

"What do you want to do tonight, then?"

"It's Friday night, so I don't have a choice."

"Is that really what you want to do?" I ask her. "Sit around the house playing Uno with your parents?"

"No," she admits, although I won't let on how many times I've enjoyed the boring sameness of their Uno game as opposed to the screaming bedlam in my house.

"You know, the other day at Kate's house, that felt like summer," I say.

"What do you mean?"

"I mean all the stuff you see on TV and movies. Isn't summer supposed to be about having a bunch of friends, laughing, and doing all the stuff you can't do during school?"

"And being stoned," Ashley adds.

"Ashley, no one's making you do anything you don't want," I remind her. "I'm not doing anything, so why should you?"

"I just hate being around people like that," she says, with that faraway look in her eyes. I know I can't convince her, so I just go silent and listen to the dogs play. For most of our friendship, Ashley and I have wanted the same things, so I don't think either of us knows how to proceed. We don't want to hurt each other's feelings, but one of us is going to have to give in. And it isn't going to be me. I'm becoming Danielle the Defiant, even to my BFF.

"Okay, I'll make a deal with you," I finally say.

"What's that?"

"Let's go over there tonight, and if you still feel the same, I'll never bring it up again."

"Deal," Ashley says, then we do the spit shake I'd shown her.

We gather up the dogs, and Ashley triple-checks the lock on the house door and the latch on the backyard gate before we exit. She won't admit it, but she's scared about taking on this responsibility. As we walk back to her house, she starts telling me about the new Holly Black novel she's reading, but I can't pay attention to fantasy fiction when I'm already living it.

"We're going out for a while," Ashley announces after she wins yet another Uno battle. I've noticed Ashley rarely asks her parents if she can do something. Instead, she just tells them her intentions and leaves it up to them to correct her, which they rarely do.

"It's pretty late," her father says. It's all of nine o'clock.

"For old people," Ashley half whispers, earning a frown from her mother.

"Where are you going?" her father asks.

I step in, as Ashley and I had agreed. She said she couldn't lie to "the 'rents," but didn't see anything wrong if I did, so I answer, "My friend Evan is taking us to a nine thirty movie."

"I see," her mother replies to my half-truth. Evan *is* picking us up, just not for a movie.

"I want you home by midnight," her father says.

"Which is too late," her mother adds, "but since you already made plans...Next time, Ashley, ask us first."

"I know," Ashley says out of the side of her mouth, trying to hide her smile.

"Do you want us to let out the Ambroses' dogs for you?" her mother asks, but before Ashley can answer, her father interrupts.

"That's her responsibility," he says. Ashley lets out a sigh, but nods in compliance.

"We should call Evan and remind him," I say, and then Ashley and I quickly leave the room. I use her cell and catch Evan just as he's leaving work. Like Ashley, he doesn't sound too interested in hanging out again at the Barker house, but it's easy for me to get Evan to do whatever I ask him. After I hang up the phone, I feel shitty about using him like this, but I also know he wants to use me. He likes me and all, but Mom's right, most boys just want one thing, and I wasn't providing it to him. I'm sure if I gave it to Evan, he'd toss me aside right after, like so many of the Dad wannabes did to Mom. One friend uses another; welcome to the summer before I turn sixteen.

• • •

We'll arrive at Reid's later than I wanted, thanks to Buster, who suddenly decides to take a swim. It takes all three of us to corral him out of the pool. As I look at my wet white T-shirt, and see Evan staring at it, I wonder if he'd thrown a toy into the pool for Buster to fetch. I want to go inside the house to find a towel, but Ashley's agitated about the noise we're making. She wants us to leave but the dogs aren't cooperating.

"I wasn't supposed to bring anybody over here with me," Ashley says, sounding furious, mostly at herself, even if she's staring at me. "I should have had you guys stay in the car."

"Blame Buster," Evan says, looking at Ashley and not at me for once.

"They said no guests, no parties," Ashley says, gritting her teeth.

"We're not guests, we're your friends," I remind her.

"And this is no party," Evan cracks. That even gets a small laugh out of Ashley.

We finally get the dogs back into the house and drive over to Reid's place. As we pull in front, I can hear music playing. Just before we get out of Evan's car, I mumble to myself, "Now *this* is a party."

"Is Reid around?" I ask the guys standing in the driveway. Evan and Ashley are still in the car, acting like they're afraid to set foot on an alien planet.

"I don't know," the guy replies, then laughs. He and two other guys are kneeling next to a jacked-up Caddy. They're drinking beer, listening to Lil Wayne, and putting on new rims.

"Be nice, she might be a friend of Reid's," guy number two mutters. "He's inside somewhere."

"Thanks," I reply, which causes all of them to laugh. Manners don't matter much here. I look back at Evan and Ashley; they're still in the car. I like my friends, but I don't understand why they won't give this a chance. Why can't they act how I want them to?

Once inside the house I notice that there are actually fewer people around than the time before, and these people seem older. There's more faint recognition of some faces, although with their glazed eyes, it's harder for them to see me. I walk around for a while by myself, picking up—but not drinking— a beer to look like everybody else. Following a trail of smoke and loud laughter, I end up on the back porch, where a small group is hanging out. I light up a cigarette, just blending in.

For a long time, nobody talks to me, not that I could hear anybody anyway over the booming rap music. No one's challenging me or wondering who I am; at the same time, nobody's really paying any attention. It's kind of like school again, except I'm at least sitting down with the cool kids being ignored, rather than standing on the outside looking in.

"Where's Reid?" I finally ask during the relative quiet between songs.

"He's everywhere," some heavily tattooed yet gorgeous girl says.

"And he's nowhere!" a tall guy with her adds, cracking everybody up.

"Are you like his daughter, or what?" Tattoo Girl quips. That gets an even bigger laugh. I feel myself blushing, so I take a quick drag on my smoke and my first swig of the beer. I try to act cool, but I gag on the nasty warm Budweiser.

"Better get her a baby bottle," Tattoo Girl says, earning another big laugh from the onlookers.

I quickly look around, wondering if Reid will rescue me again or if this is a test.

"*You'll* need a baby bottle, honey, no way you could breast-feed with those," I shout back, pointing at Tattoo Girl's unfilled black beater.

"Oh, snap!" somebody shouts, then more laughter.

"More than a mouthful is wasted," Tattoo Guy says, pulling Tattoo Girl closer to him.

After that, people, including the inked couple, start talking *to* me rather than *around* me. They talk mostly about cars, jobs they used to have or want to find, and getting apartments away from their parents. Every now and then, some classic heavy metal song blares out and everybody stops talking to sing along. It's during one of these group sing-alongs, to Metallica's "Enter the Sandman," that Reid appears on the back porch.

Our eyes meet, then mine immediately dart back toward the ground. He walks over to me. Like everybody else, he's got a smoke in one hand and a beer in the other, although he's the only one drinking a Heineken: everybody else is sticking with Bud. I feel a cold sweat wash over my body in the June heat, unsure what I'm supposed to say or do in front of all these people. I wait for Reid.

"Everybody, meet Danielle," he says to the group. He puts his hand on my arm, but doesn't lean in to kiss me.

"Hey," the group says in unison.

"She's a friend of Vic's," Reid says, then laughs. "I told you Vic still had a purpose."

It gets a laugh, but I'm dying inside. I'm not his girlfriend; I'm a friend of someone he doesn't even like. I finish off my smoke, trying not to look at Reid's green eyes, which push me away instead of pulling me in. I've gone from hot to cool to cold.

"Hey, look at me," Reid whispers in my ear, rubbing up against me. "I was hoping you'd get here before everybody so we could have some time alone."

"I'm sorry," I whisper back. My mouth's close to his face; I want to kiss him, but I can sense that's not what he wants. At least not right here and now.

"What happened?" he asks.

I tell him the story about Buster's sudden desire for a night swim. It's hard for him to pay attention, not just because of the music, but because everybody wants a second of his time, either in person or on his always-ringing cell. It takes forever to finish the story, and while he's looking at me, it doesn't seem like he's listening. He isn't really listening to anybody, and so the porch soon clears out, except for Tattoo Girl and her boy. Reid's yawning when he interrupts me. "Night swimming is so cool."

I'm looking into his green eyes as my mind calculates the

cost of betrayal against the rewards of romance. "We could go over there, if you want," I say softly.

"Night swim pool party," Reid says to Tattoo Girl and Boy. He puts out his cigarette on the porch, smashing the butt under his foot, and picks up a six-pack of beer from the cooler.

"Cool," Tattoo Girl says to Reid. She gives me an "it's all good" nod. Before I can say anything else, the tattoo couple head into the house, leaving me and Reid alone.

Reid turns around and puts out his hand, motioning me to join him. He grabs my hand and pulls me next to him. Seconds later, when he kisses me, it's like all the air goes out of my body and into his. I wrap my arms around him as he pulls me tighter and whispers in my ear, "So, where's this pool party going down?"

"We're not taking all these people to . . ."

"Don't worry, I won't let you get in trouble."

"It's more my friend Ashley that—" Before I can finish, Reid interrupts me.

"Hey, Wayne, we're taking your wheels," he shouts into the house.

"It's always *my* wheels," Wayne says, sticking his head back out on the porch. "I'm not cool enough to drive the Viper."

"No one's cool enough but me," Reid laughs, then hands me the six-pack from the cooler. "It's the black Impala behind the house. Meet me there after I clear out the trash."

I watch as Reid strolls over to the main stereo in the living room. He turns it off, and at first there's a lot of "who the fuck did that" grumbling, but it quickly ends when people see it's Reid.

"What's going on, dude?" one of the longhairs who'd been out front asks.

"Party's over, clear out," Reid says. "If you don't like it, Brandon, don't come back."

"Dude, I was just saying," Brandon says, almost stuttering.

"Somebody get those wannabes from the basement," Reid says to no one in particular.

"Dude, I'm on it!" Brandon shouts, running off in record time.

As people leave, I look for Evan and Ashley, who are standing outside of Evan's car. Standing with them is Angie, the prettier of the blond basement girls from the other day.

"So you're Vic's brother?" I hear Angie say to Evan as I join them by the car.

"I plead guilty," Evan replies.

"Well, you won't find him around here anymore. Reid and Vic are on the outs," Angie says before I shut her up with my best evil glare.

"Reid?" Ashley asks Angie, but she's looking at me.

"Yeah, Reid Barker. This is his house. He lives here with his mom," Angie adds.

"Kate doesn't live here?" Ashley says, still talking to Angie but staring straight at me.

"She's with her dad someplace for the summer," Angie

answers. I feel like the front porch is sinking and water's rushing in all around.

"Reid Barker," Ashley says with disgust. It was only a matter of time: the truth is a seed that's always ready to sprout. You can kick dirt on it, but it keeps growing toward the light.

"I'm getting a ride home with someone else," I tell Ashley.

"I'm sure you are," Ashley replies.

"Reid's so cool," Angie butts in. "Plus, he's really sexy."

I bite my bottom lip, but can't keep my mouth shut. "What do you mean?"

"Great kisser, the best ever," Angie says, then raises her overplucked eyebrows.

My face flushes fire-engine red; there's a siren screaming in my heart.

"You his girlfriend or something?" Evan asks Angie, totally oblivious to me for once.

"I'm a friend," she says, then winks. "With benefits."

"Some friend," Ashley mumbles to me. "Some benefit."

I don't even bother to say goodbye to Ashley or Evan, or scream "lying bitch" at Angie, before I bolt. I mix in with the dispersing crowd, but I don't head toward the street. Instead, I circle behind the house to the alley. I catch my breath, make sure that Evan or Ashley haven't followed me, then open up one of the Heinekens. It tastes less foul than the Budweiser, but it still can't blot out the bitter taste in my mouth. I take one sip and hurl the bottle against the curb; it shatters into a hundred pieces and showers the littered alley with alcohol. I stare up at the moon, a little crescent moon like Reid's smile mocking me, and know I'm headed back to the lonely loveless life that losers like me deserve.

• • •

I've walked maybe a quarter of a mile away from Reid's house when I hear, "Hey, you want a ride?" It's Tattoo Girl, yelling from the open window of the Impala, which has pulled up next to me.

I pretend not to hear her voice, or the car slowing down. The metal music blasts out of the car, but Reid shouts over it. "What's wrong?"

I wipe my nose and try to hide my stupid schoolgirl tears, but I keep walking.

"Come on, be cool," Reid says. "We were waiting for you, but Angie said you split."

"She would know," I snap. The car stops, and Reid emerges from the backseat.

"What does that mean?" he asks. His arms are outstretched; mine remain at my side.

"She's your friend with benefits, right?" I shoot back.

"What the hell are you talking about?" Reid says. He's not shocked; in fact, he acts like he's trying not to laugh at me. "Who told you that?"

"She did," I answer with my arms crossed over my chest.

"She wishes," he says, then laughs. "Angie has quite an imagination."

I'm feeling stupid, so I glance away from him. "Then she's not..."

"Look at me, Danielle. Angie's nothing," he reassures me. "She's pissed from the other day and stirring up drama. You know how wannabes like her are, right? She's jealous of you."

"Really?" I ask, wiping my nose again.

"Angie isn't anything to me," Reid says. "Trust me on that."

I stumble over what to say, flashing back across years of me screaming at my mother, "Trust me," and her refusing to do so. Maybe it's my turn to be better than her and believe. I let Reid pull me slowly toward him, allowing a gentle kiss, not a spit shake, to seal the deal.

Reid grabs my hand as we head back to the car. "Hey, where's my Heinies?"

I look away from him, knowing this is a moment in time that I'll always regret. He'll be angry, leave me, and I'll be nothing again. I'll be as broken as that beer bottle. "Reid, I..."

"Don't worry about it. There's more than one way to party," he says as we reach Big Wayne's black Impala, which shakes from the pounding bass.

"You wanna drive?" Reid asks.

"I don't know how to drive," I reply. Yet another uncool confession.

"We'll most certainly have to do something about that," he says, then crawls into the car, pulling me in behind him. As soon as we sit down, he lights up a Newport, takes a drag, then puts it into my mouth.

"So where to?" Wayne asks. I still don't know his girl-friend's name, but suspect it might be found among Wayne's numerous tats.

I give directions, then Reid whispers, "Don't worry, every-thing's cool."

I listen to the music and the tattoo lovers' laughter, and in my heart, I know Reid's right.

. . .

I ask Wayne to turn down the music when we pull onto Ash-ley's street. We drive by her house. I see her light's on, so I know she made it home safe. I'm sure Mom's cursing herself for tak-ing away my cell phone since it's well past midnight and I'm way past curfew, and she's no doubt already called Ashley. I wonder if Ashley lied for me, especially after I've lied so much to her. As I unhook the latch at the Ambrose house, I wonder how many lies a friendship can stand.

The dogs bark as we settle in by the pool, but stop after a while. When no lights come on in the nearby houses and no sirens start screaming across the sky, I figure we're safe. We all sit at the far end of the pool, the coolness of the water taking the heat off this hot-blooded evening. I hang with Reid; I have nothing to say to Wayne or his girlfriend, who he called Becca.

After about twenty minutes, Reid calls Wayne over, whis-pering into his ear. Wayne cracks up, then he and Becca head down to the other end of the pool, strip off what little clothing they're wearing, and jump in. I try not to stare at their naked bodies, but it's hard. Wayne yells, "All right!" which gets the dogs barking and Reid glaring.

For a while, the only noise other than chirping crickets is the sound of Wayne and Becca splashing and kissing. Even though there's no music playing, this feels like I'm living in a music video instead of my life.

"You guys getting in?" Wayne yells, triggering another glare from Reid and another round of barking from the dogs.

Reid shakes his head, then winks at me. "Wayne's got shit for brains."

I don't say anything. I'm too busy trying to block out the sounds of the dogs and the sight of Becca's naked tattooed back, which is now covering most of Wayne's naked tattooed front.

"I guess if you smoke a bag of shit a day, then that's what happens."

"I guess," I reply.

"Bakers shouldn't eat their own donuts," Reid says. He laughs and then winks again. I don't get it but laugh anyway. Every time I laugh at something Reid says, he breaks out that smile, which makes me feel more comfortable. It's like I'm coasting and the hill is behind me.

After the dogs quiet down, Reid takes off his shirt, shoes, pants, and socks. I try looking everywhere but at him as he does a huge dive into the pool, splashing me with water.

"You coming in?" he asks, splashing more water toward me.

I shake my head. I don't want to say no to him, but I can't say yes.

"You sure?" he asks under the rain of more splashes.

"I don't know how to swim," I say, which is half-true. I don't want to be in the water with my clothes on, and I'm not going to jump in with my clothes off, not with Wayne nearby.

"Don't know how to swim or drive," Reid says, shooting me that smile. "I gotta lot of stuff to teach you."

Before I can say anything, Reid swims toward me and starts running his right hand up my leg. I'm as embarrassed by my body as I am by the nearly naked body two feet in front of me. I notice for the first time the spiderweb-like tattoo at the top of his back.

"Hey, light me up," he says, pointing toward the pack of smokes on the table. I turn to get the smokes and his lighter.

"Here," I say, putting the cigarette in front of me, but his hands remain in the water.

"Put it in my mouth," he says with a smile. I do as he asks, then bend over to light it, my hands shaking like it was January, not June.

"I'm sorry."

"For what?" Reid says, as I unsuccessfully flick the lighter.

"For being so clumsy, for not being cool," I mutter. Another useless flick.

"Danielle, I think you're hot," he says, steadying my hands with his.

"Then you must be really wasted."

"No. You're so hot, I think you need to cool down," he says, grasping my right wrist and pulling me into the pool. I scream in shock, but the barking of the dogs and the laughter—of Wayne, Becca, and especially Reid—are soon the loudest sounds of all.

"Wait here," Reid whispers, then he swims to the center of the pool. He motions for Wayne to come over and says something in his ear. Wayne laughs, then says something back to Reid. He and Becca gather their clothes, get dressed, and head out to the car, while Reid swims to me.

"What's going on?" I ask him.

"You and me," he says. We splash around in the water, but most of the time, Reid's hands are rubbing up against my body, not slapping the water. After a while, Reid crawls out, then sits on one of the lounge chairs, turning it so its back faces the gate.

"Come here," he says. I leave the water to stand before him shivering in my wet clothes.

"How could you be cold when you're so smokin' hot?" he asks. I'm even more embarrassed at my body's natural reactions, which all seem very new, strange, and exciting.

I don't even know what to say to this. I really want to look away, but I know that's not what he wants.

"From what I can see, you're one sexy woman, but I'd love to see more. Don't worry, Wayne and Becca are taking a little walk on the outside," he says in the sexiest voice I've ever heard. I know this is my cue. I take off the wet T-shirt.

"Very sexy," he purrs, and I toss the T-shirt at him. He catches it, laughs, then sits up in the chair and whispers through his smile, "That's from what I can see."

I reach behind and unhook my bra, which seems to take forever as my clumsiness feeds my nervousness. Just as if I was in the locker room at school, I kneel down to cover up, which causes Reid to laugh. His laughter and his smile are intoxicating, and I drop my arms along with my doubts and fears.

"Very hot, very sexy," he says as he moves toward me. He kisses the top of my head, my mouth, my neck, and then my breasts. Hot sweet sensations shoot from the center of my body toward my brain and below. I'm breathing heavily, but Reid's acting so relaxed.

"Everything about you is hot," he says, kissing the top of my head again. I try to crawl closer to him, but instead he puts his hand on my shoulder. He drops my T-shirt in front of me, by my knees, at the foot of the lounge chair, and whispers, "Especially your mouth."

I don't say anything, but he says, "Look at me, Danielle. It's just me and you, just like you always wanted." He circles my mouth with his index finger, and then puts it inside. He kisses the top of my head again, then stands, taking off his wet underwear. Sitting back in the lounge chair, he puts his hands behind his head and says, "Why don't you show me that sexy mouth in action?"

Before I can make a move, I hear Wayne shout, "Dude, fuck it, we're busted!"

Reid pushes me away, then looks at Wayne, who's standing by the gate. As I quickly put my clothes back on, I see Wayne pointing to the house next door. All its lights are now on; flashing red lights are sure to follow. But the sight of Reid's sexy bare ass in front of me quickly stops me from looking anywhere else.

"Keys!" Reid yells as he finishes putting on his clothes quickly. I'm terrified, almost shaking, but I can tell Reid's icy calm. Wayne reaches into his pocket, then tosses Reid the keys to his car as we run toward the gate. "Let's roll!"

I latch the gate behind us, then jump in the already running car. Reid's in the driver's seat, with Wayne next to him. I join Becca in the back. I must look embarrassed, and I'm even more so when she hands me a stick of gum. Reid hits the gas, leaving a patch of rubber on the pavement, an angry rumble of barking dogs, and maybe the best night of my fifteen-year-old life behind us.

7

SATURDAY, JUNE 28

"You promised, remember?" Ashley says over the sounds of three crazed barking dogs.

"I know," I say through a yawn. I didn't sleep much last night thinking about Reid, but I still managed to get up early and bike over to Ashley's house first thing in the morning. We walked mostly in angry silence over to the Ambrose house. I want to apologize, but my other motive is to pick up the cigarette butts from our improvised pool party last night.

"I'm not going over to Reid's house again," Ashley says over her shoulder. She's feeding the dogs, which gives me time to pocket the evidence.

"But, Ashley," I start.

"You take us there, ditch us yet again, and then leave without us," she says. "What's going on with you?"

"Nothing," I reply, avoiding her glare.

"You're not seeing him again, are you?" she asks.

I start walking toward the other end of the pool, then say, "You don't have to go."

"You'll only get hurt," Ashley says sharply as she and the dogs follow me.

"I guess there's one way not to get hurt," I say.

"What's that?"

"Never fall in love," I shoot back, wondering why I'm so angry at Ashley, wondering more where within me the word "love" came from.

"You think you know everything, but you don't know anything," Ashley says.

"What does that mean?" I ask, almost shouting at her.

"Like you say, Danny: whatever." Ashley then walks away from me. I don't blame her.

"Look, I'm sorry," I say.

"Evan's really upset too," Ashley adds.

"Why?"

"Because he likes you, Danny."

"I know," I mutter, ashamed to admit it. Rejecting him is one thing, but I know I'm doing more: it feels like I'm betraying him. I don't like to hurt anyone's feelings, but especially not Evan's since he *is* such a nice guy.

"He's not going over there anymore," she says. "And you know, you shouldn't either."

"You sound like your mother," I crack back, hoping to raise a smile, but all I get in return is a deep, angry stare.

"You don't know anything about my mother," she says harshly.

"I don't want to get in a fight with you, Ash, I'm sorry," I say, trying to calm her down.

"Don't talk about my mother," she snaps again.

"What is wrong with you?" I ask her, but as she's done so many times in the past, Ashley answers with silence. Even though she's my best friend, sometimes I feel like I've got only a broad outline of her. Like she's a figure in a coloring book, and I have to fill her in as best I can with the colors she lets me see.

Finally she speaks, but not to me. "Let's go, boys!" The dogs run toward her. They're jumping all over her, like a long-lost friend, even as her best friend forever is slithering away from her.

• • •

Before I leave Ashley's house, I use her phone to call Reid, but he doesn't pick up. I bike home, try calling him again without success, and then decide to go visit him. He's probably out back working on the Viper. But before I see him, I have to get ready. It's hard for me to believe that Reid thinks I'm hot, but all this biking is dropping off those remaining baby-fat and Halo Burger pounds. This morning, rather than putting on yet another ill-fitting T-shirt, I pick out a tight white beater I'd bought in the spring but never felt right about wearing. Instead of my torn jeans, I put on some army surplus pants I've chopped into shorts, and top it off with a flaming red bandanna. I might still be riding my bike, but I know I don't look like some stupid kid anymore.

Reid's Viper isn't in front of his house when I get there, but there's a black Mustang on the street and a huge GMC pickup truck that nearly fills the whole driveway. I put my bike down in the front yard, tuck in my shirt to make it tighter, then apply some last-second sparkly lip gloss before I knock on the door. No one answers. I knock louder. After a while, I hear some noise on the other side, and the door slowly opens.

"Is Reid home?" I ask the woman who answers the door.

"I don't know," is her less than helpful response. Her voice is sandpaper-rough and her eyes are barely open. She's wearing dark coveralls, like my dad used to wear when he worked at one of the GM plants. "Maybe he's sleeping, which is what I want to be doing."

"Just tell—" Before I can finish, she shuts the door. I wait down the street for about a half hour, but nobody emerges from the house. Stranger yet, nobody's coming over to Reid's just to hang out. Nobody but me. Alone again.

. . .

I bike over to the Capitol to get something to eat. Mom's mad that I came in late, but believed the story I'd made up about fighting with Ashley, then walking home. She even believed my explanation of the wet clothing; I told her I'd cut through the driving range down the street when the sprinklers turned on. My guess is she's so used to my being moody and clumsy that she'll believe those lies rather than the truth. Not that I'll ever tell her that.

Mom's workday is just starting, and it looks to be a busy one. The truck plant near the Capitol is one of the few Flint auto factories still open and running three shifts all seven days.

I sit at the table with the other waitresses. Most of them are

Mom's age, and as I've learned through the years, they all have almost the same story: at least one divorce, child support checks that never arrive on time or ever, unemployed boyfriends, two jobs, and three packs a day. As I listen to these women in their black Capitol polo shirts talking about their lives, I vow I'll become an A student for the rest of high school. I love my mom, but I don't want her life.

I borrow some of Mom's tip money and use the pay phone to call both Evan and Ashley, just to talk to someone. Neither of them pick up, but even if they did, I wouldn't really know what to say to them. They'd want to go to a movie, bookstore, or maybe the mall, but I just want to be at Reid's house.

After a while, I decide to try Reid again. He answers after the tenth ring.

"Hey, what's up?" he asks, then coughs.

"I was over earlier," I tell him. "Your mom was kind of rude to me."

"When she's like that, just avoid her," he says. In the background, I can hear rustling.

"Why don't you move out?" I ask him.

I hear a lighter click. Reid says, "Normally she leaves me alone, and I leave her alone. I don't have to pay rent, so I can spend all my money on my car and my friends. But now she's on one of her benders, and bent the shit out of shape, especially after the last party."

"What do you mean?"

"Somebody busted something at the house the other night,

so she's all pissed off," Reid says, then coughs. "Don't think we'll be partying at my house for a while."

"Okay," I say, still waiting for him to invite me over.

"Probably best," he says. "Too many wannabes and hangers-on."

I wonder if he means Angie.

"Hey, lots of my friends are jerks. They're not cool like you," Reid says. "They don't understand me like you. They come over, drink my beer, play with my shit, and do business."

"Business?"

Reid pauses, coughs, then says, "Besides, I want you all to myself, baby."

"Whatever you want, Reid."

"Girls like Angie, they're real jealous types," he continues. "Real shit-stirrers."

"I understand," I say, which isn't totally true.

"So, I'm just protecting you from all that shit."

"Okay, Reid."

"Make sure you call first," he says. "You don't want to run into my drunk mom again."

"Okay," I mutter again. I've read how love leaves you speechless, and I'm living proof.

"So, where you at?" he asks.

"Just hanging out where my mom works," I shout over the loud shift-change rush.

"Where's that?"

"The Capitol on Bristol," I answer, almost wincing. If he

wants to come over here, my mom will want to meet him, and I'm so not ready for that.

"I got no wheels now," Reid says. He coughs out phlegm while I breathe a sigh of relief. "I gave Vic another shot. He's putting new speakers in the Viper, but he's taking forever."

"I could bike over," I say, but I really want to ask what the deal between Reid and Vic is.

"Why don't you drive over?"

"I don't know how to drive, remember?" I say gently.

"I'll teach you," he says. "I'll get Big Wayne to give me a ride down there. Stay put."

"I don't want to drive Wayne's car."

"He wouldn't let you touch The Mighty Impala," Reid says with a laugh.

"Then how can you teach me to drive?" I ask. "What car are we gonna use?"

"Your mom's," Reid says, then laughs again before he hangs up the phone.

· · ·

Before I head toward the parking lot, I ask Mom when her shift's over and make sure she's not running errands during her breaks. If she's suspicious, she doesn't let on, even when I ask to get some gum from her purse. I do take some gum, but that's not all I take.

After about ten minutes, I go outside. Reid's leaning on the hood of Wayne's car, smoking a Newport, wearing a long blue

T-shirt, and blocking out the glare of the sun with a pair of new sunglasses that look like they have diamonds in the tips. "You got the keys?"

I nod, and he puts out his hands.

"Throw 'em," he commands. I send Mom's keys flying across the parking lot. Reid catches them, laughs, and walks toward me. He shouts something to Wayne, who laughs and then peels out of the lot, adding to its huge collection of tire marks.

"Which one?"

I point at the blue-and-rust-colored Malibu with shame, thinking about Reid's cold-as-hell Viper and Wayne's cool Impala. I can tell Reid's trying not to laugh as he unlocks the doors and climbs in the passenger's seat. I take the unfamiliar spot behind the wheel.

"First rule of driving," Reid says, showing me a CD, "is having the right music."

He puts the key in the ignition, and then pushes the CD into the player. Even through Mom's crappy crackling speakers, AC/DC's "Highway to Hell" sounds fine.

Reid shouts his driving instructions over the music. I manage not to hit anything in the parking lot, not to kill us pulling onto Van Slyke Road, and not to smash into the car in front of us at the stop light on Bristol Road. All the time, my teeth are clenched with fear, while my heart's beating faster at the touch of Reid's hand on my arm, helping me steer safely. He makes me drive around the block a few times, then dares me to take it out on the expressway.

"The key to merging is very simple," he says with great seriousness as we start down the entrance ramp from Bristol onto I-75 north.

"What's that?" I ask. I need the confidence of his eyes, but his sunglasses and my fear of taking my eyes off the road present a double obstacle.

"Drive like hell!" he shouts, then pushes his hand down hard on my leg, causing the engine to race and our speed to scream up to almost seventy in just a few seconds. My heart plummets into my stomach; butterflies are crashing into each other and I try not to crash into the cars in front of me. "Drive like hell, Danielle, drive like hell!"

He clicks the CD twice and "Highway to Hell" repeats. My hands are still shaking, but having Reid's arm around my shoulder helps distract me from the pit of fear in my gut. We drive just a few miles north on I-75, then I exit back onto safer city streets. I get ready to turn onto Bristol, but Reid tells me to head to his house. He keeps telling me what a great job I'm doing and how he can't wait to teach me to drive the Viper. I somehow get to his house without killing either of us.

We're sitting in his driveway. His mom's truck is nowhere in sight. Reid's arm is off my shoulder. Now he's leaning against me, his hand almost in my lap.

"I need to bring the car back," I say. "My mom's shift is over soon."

"Don't worry about that," he says, then pulls me tight. Words stick in my throat as his hand moves up from my lap until his fingers pass over my right breast. I should roll down the car windows because they're starting to steam up.

"We didn't really get started the other night," he whispers as the long fingers of his right hand run down my shirt, every now and then lightly brushing against my breasts. "Let's go inside."

"My mom would kill me," I say, embarrassed even as the words leave my mouth.

"I wonder if being dead is better than being tortured," he says as he takes my hand and rubs them over the small scars on his arm. "I've lived through so much shit in my life."

"Reid, I'm so sorry."

"I need somebody who understands me like you do," Reid says, pulling up his sleeve. He points at his scars. "I need somebody to help me heal all this shit."

"Reid, it's just—," I start, but his kiss stops me from speaking.

"I need you," Reid says, almost pleading as he opens up the passenger door. He walks slowly, head down, toward his front door, then turns, looks at me, and walks inside. I sit in the car for a moment, rearranging my clothes and my thoughts. The steam might evaporate, but the heat doesn't. The front door to his house remains open, and seconds later, the driver's door of my mom's Malibu opens too, as I start the long walk toward Reid's house. I've stolen Mom's car, Reid's stolen my heart, and I'm ready for him to take whatever else he needs.

8

SATURDAY, JULY 12

"Where have you been hiding?" Evan asks. It's a question he, Ashley, and my mother have all been asking for the last two weeks. I've resurfaced to see Evan at the mall before I head downtown to the library to meet up with Ashley for book club.

"I've just been hanging out," I say slowly. Where I've really been—with Reid, whenever he's not too busy—is not something Evan wants to know. He wouldn't like it, but mostly he wouldn't understand it, in part because I can't really explain it. It's not about anything Reid says, does, or gives me. It's more about how I feel when I'm with him.

"Hanging out like an apple waiting to be picked." Evan sounds pretty self-righteous for a guy sweating under an ugly red Halo Burger hat. His awkwardness makes me sigh.

"Whatever," I say. I knew meeting up with Evan was a mistake, but I'm trying to maintain our friendship, and I also want Mom to keep thinking that he's my boyfriend. "How about you?" I ask in the most friendly manner I can summon.

"You've been at Reid's, I know it," he says with an icy tone.

"No," I answer, which isn't a total lie. Reid and I spend some time at his house, but mostly we've driving around, either in the Viper or in Mom's "borrowed" Malibu. She's yet to discover that we're taking her wheels while she works.

"He's no good. You know that, right?" Evan's voice cracks.

"Just because he and Vic don't like each other, that—"

"I don't even like my brother, so this has nothing to do with him," Evan cuts me off.

"Jealous," I whisper under my breath.

"I don't think so," Evan says, trying to sound confident.

"Really?" I arch the eyebrow that—if everything goes as planned—I'll be getting pierced tonight by Becca, after which the four of us will stay the whole night at Reid's. The party ban is lifted at his house, so everybody's coming over. Everybody but Evan, Ashley, and Vic.

Evan scratches his whisker-free chin and says, "Maybe I am jealous. Paint me green like it's St. Patrick's Day and I'll be your leprechaun of love."

I try hard not to laugh, but I'm way too tired.

"You think I'm real funny," Evan says. "At school, I'm funny enough to laugh with, but now you're laughing at me. I'm the one who should be laughing at you."

"What do you mean?"

"You should talk to Vic about Reid, he's got lots of stories to tell. Most of them are about girls Reid fucked, then fucked over."

"You're just saying that," I shoot back, angry at myself for reaching out to him. I want us to stay friends, but I guess if I can't be his girlfriend, then I can only be his enemy.

"Ask Vic about how Reid gets his money," Evan continues. "Or ask him yourself."

"Maybe I could ask Vic why Reid doesn't want him hanging out there anymore," I snap back. "Maybe I could ask Vic why he's such a loser. Just like his brother."

"Fine, Danielle," Evan says, then stands up. "I've got to go work at a real job."

"Fine yourself," I say, pushing the tray of half-eaten food across the table at him.

"You should take that advice," Evan says as he picks up the tray. "You should *find* yourself, because I think you're lost."

"You are so annoying." I start to walk away, but he grabs my hand.

"You're right, I'm annoying, but you know what else I am?" he asks. He lets my hand drop as I pretend not to hear him say, "I'm somebody who cares and doesn't want you hurt."

· · ·

I'm sitting on the bus enjoying the new Lil Wayne on a sweet iPod Nano that Reid gave me. I'm trying to let the music distract me, but it's not working. I'm not sure why, but Evan's got me all upset, mostly because of the things I wish I'd said to him. He's wrong: I *have* found myself, found myself in Reid's eyes. Before this summer, when I looked in a mirror I saw this lumpy,

awkward outsider. But when Reid sees me, he sees someone different. He sees a hot girl who he wants to be with. When I'm
with him, I don't feel like Danielle the Dork, I feel like Danielle
the Desirable.

In some ways, though, I'm more frustrated than ever because
there's nobody I can tell. I almost want to grab one of these ran-
dom people on the bus and make them listen to me. I can't tell
Mom, Evan, or even Ashley about Reid. They all disapprove for
one reason or another, mostly because they're jealous. Friends
and family always say they want you to be happy, but I'm wondering now if that's just another lie. They only want me to be
happy, if it's on their terms.

I meet Ashley in front of the library a few minutes before
book club starts. I showed up as late as I could because after
Evan's lunch lecture, I didn't need another one from Ashley.
She's wearing her "Give Peace a Chance" T-shirt, and I wonder
if that's some subtle message. But she surprises me by acting like
everything's fine and we start talking like old times, until I
notice that something's wrong. This isn't me; it's who I used
to be.

Book club is strange. Unlike last year, when I read every
book cover to cover, I hadn't finished the book, *Beauty*. I still
said a few things I remembered about another book by Robin
McKinley, but it seemed like Ashley was always trying to top
or contradict the few things I did say. Whenever Mike or
David spoke, though, Ashley was telling them how great their
comments were.

After book club, Ashley and I wait for her mom by the Longway Planetarium. It's a hot day, and we have our shoes off, cooling our feet in the small reflecting pool behind the building. We talk about a lot of stuff, but I never mention Reid, even though that's all I want to talk about.

Knowing Ashley's mom would be right on time, not a minute too soon or too late, I wait until almost the last moment to say something serious. "Ashley, I need a favor."

"CliffsNotes for the next book," she cracks as she splashes water my way.

"Can I spend the night at your house tonight?" I ask.

"It's about time," Ashley says.

"You're sure it's okay?" I ask very slowly.

"I'll just tell the 'rents," she says. "They like you, Danielle. My mom even asked why you weren't hanging out as much. She was all scared we'd had a fight or something."

"BFFs never fight," I say. Then I splash water back at her.

"Wrong! Splash fight!" Ashley yells. I let out a loud laugh as we kick our legs wildly in the water, like people drowning. But when I catch a glimpse of myself in the reflecting pool, I think about how long I felt like *I* was underwater, until Reid pulled me out and resuscitated me.

• • •

It's around ten when we hear the door to her parents' room close. Ashley's got a whole pile of science fiction and fantasy DVDs. She's settling in for the evening.

"What do you want to watch first?" she asks.

"Ash, I need another favor," I say.

"What's that?"

"I can trust you, right?" She nods in agreement. "I'm not really going to spend the night here."

"What do you mean?" she asks.

"I'm going over to Reid's tonight," I say, biting my lip even as I speak the words.

"But you said you were . . ."

"Ashley, I'm sorry, but I need you to cover for me. It will—"

But she cuts me off. "I'm cold." She sits on her bed, and starts rocking herself for comfort.

"Please, just this one time."

"No, it won't be one time," she hisses. "You'll want me to cover for you again and again and again. Pretty soon, you won't ask, you'll just assume that I'll cover for you and your lies."

"Ashley, please," I beg.

"I'm not going to do it," she says, shaking her head violently back and forth.

"Best friends forever," I counter, pulling rank.

"A friend doesn't ask a friend to lie," she says, then stares at me.

"One time." I'm almost shouting now.

"Once the lies start, they never fucking end," Ashley hisses again.

I'm in silent shock. I've never heard Ashley drop the f-bomb anywhere anytime.

"Until you fucking die," she says, curling up in a ball in the corner of her bed.

"Ashley, what's going on?" I ask.

"What the fuck do you care?" she shouts.

"Where is this coming from?" I try to edge closer, but her angry eyes push me back.

"Get out of my sight!" she says, throwing a pillow in my direction.

"Ashley, look, I'm sorry." I start to cry, but Ashley, as always, holds her tears inside.

"Just leave me, like everybody else," she says, her back—and her heart—turned away from me.

I try to speak again, but no words come. Quickly and quietly, I gather up my overnight bag, then tiptoe like a thief down the stairs and out the door.

I wait for Reid outside of Ashley's for a long time since I can't call him. I don't get my cell back until next week. My first call will be to Ashley, and I hope she'll still talk to me. I don't know what she'll do tonight if Mom calls; I don't know what she'll say if her parents ask where I am. As I stand in the dark, I imagine something worse. Maybe I don't know Ashley at all.

But my dark thoughts scatter when Reid arrives. We kiss, but he seems distracted. We don't talk much on the ride out to his house; we just listen to music booming like a tidal wave over us. "Some weird stuff going on," he finally says. "Maybe it'd be better if you lie low until people leave."

"Reid, did I do something, because—" He cuts off my doubts with a kiss.

"I gotta do a little business first," Reid says the minute we pull into his driveway.

I nod, then lean to kiss him again, but he backs away. We climb from the car.

"Meet me in the alley in an hour," he says. Then he takes off for the garage and leaves me alone.

I shrug, smile, and head toward the alley. There are only a few cars I recognize from before, but one stands out: Vic's junker. I watch Reid go into the garage, following far behind. The door facing the alley's cracked open, and I lean in to listen. It's easy to hear since the normally cool Reid is shouting. "Vic, I told you to stay away from here!"

"It's your fault I lost my job," Vic shouts back. "I want compensation."

"You lost your job because you're an idiot!"

"I lost my job because I was a thief," Vic counters.

"Face it, Vic, you're just a loser," Reid says sharply.

"I lost my job stealing shit for you. You got so fucking much, Reid, give me something!"

"I'll give you something," Reid shouts. "I'll give you ten fucking seconds to get the hell out of here. If you ever come back, I'll kick your ass. I've done it before, I can do it again."

"You don't scare me anymore," Vic says, but the quavering tone trumps his words.

I don't wait for Vic to leave before I bolt back into the alley. I light up a Camel, but it doesn't calm me down.

When Reid doesn't come out, I go inside. I hang out with other people most of the night. Reid's busy taking calls and being the center of the storm. I think twenty times of calling Ashley, begging her to get her mom to pick me up and save me from myself. But I never make that call. After the last person leaves, around two in the morning, I join Reid in the basement for our first night together.

"Just a crazy night," Reid says as he lies down on the sofa. "But you'll make it all right."

"Really?" I ask before I kneel down.

"You know why?" he asks, then kisses the top of my head. "'Cuz you're the best ever."

9

SATURDAY, JULY 19, AND SUNDAY, JULY 20

"Danielle, are you ready to go?" Mom shouts at me.

"Almost," I mumble. As we prepare for our trip to Traverse City for my cousin's wedding, I'm hoping that Mom won't quiz Ashley and me about all the things that I've told her the two of us have done this summer. I know Ashley's still mad at me from our fight last weekend, and all the time I spend with Reid. Her coming on the trip shows she takes this best-friend stuff as seriously as I do. How friends and families fight, then forgive each other, is one of the great mysteries of nature. Once again, one of Ashley's oracle pronouncements is totally true: "You can forgive a person for anything if you love them enough."

"Ashley's mother has called twice wondering why we're late," Mom says as I hurry into my room to pack my things, including a hot new red dress Reid bought me. In the week that's passed since I spent the night with him, we've actually had some normal boyfriend-girlfriend time together, although I don't think we've been on what anyone would call a date.

When we go out together, we usually drive—sometimes with me behind the wheel, if it's Mom's car and not the Viper—out to one of the lakes north of Flint, or south around Pontiac. I'll hang around one of the malls, while Reid goes off someplace. When he comes back, he takes me shopping and buys me things like that red dress. I told Mom that I got it at Goodwill. When she asked, "Do they have one in my size?" I managed to keep it together, but all this lying to Mom is exhausting.

She *needs* to shop more at Goodwill, because Carl's back, with his hand deep in Mom's purse and his ass firmly planted on the sofa. Things seem better between them. I've only picked up the phone to order pizza, not dial 911. Neither of them is drinking, but they're both smoking more and spending more time in the bedroom with the music turned up loud. Mom's even watching him play softball, making the ultimate female sacrifice for her man.

The drive up north to Traverse City is dull. I'm sure if we were with Ashley's parents, they'd have had us playing word games or singing songs. Instead, Carl and Mom mostly ignore us, and I'm enjoying the summer air blowing through the windows and pushing the loud '90s metal music outside. Ashley and I talk for a while, about nothing much. I think about Reid because I don't want to do anything else.

My cousin Brittney's wedding is fancy, and I'm totally embarrassed. Although Mom, Ashley, and I got dressed up, Carl refused. While every other man is wearing a suit, Carl looks like a loser in his Harley T-shirt, blue jeans, and wallet chained to his belt. He's worse at the reception, drinking too much and constantly yelling at the band to play Aerosmith.

Brittney's more beautiful than ever, but the happier she looks, the sadder I get. There are not a lot of people here our age, so mostly Ashley and I dance with each other. A couple of creepy thirty-year-old guys keep hitting on us, but I don't need anyone's lame lines or leers.

Carl isn't the only one drinking, but I notice the alcohol consumption is mainly on our side of the family. My grandmother came up from Florida for the wedding, but since she and Mom don't speak, I feel like I'd be betraying my mom if I even talk to Grandma, who's a stranger to me anyway. Brittney's new husband has this big happy family who smile for the cameras like they're in some TV ad. Brittney's dad gathers us for family photos, but his wife and my mom are such different sisters: the waitress and the doctor's wife. And there's so much bad blood; my mom hasn't spoken to her mother since just after I was born. No, this wedding isn't exactly a celebration for *my* family, and I suspect that worse times are coming as Carl keeps shouting at the band. Mom says something to him, but he turns away, pushing her as he tries to balance himself.

"He's drunk," Ashley says, not even trying to hide her anger and disgust.

"You think?" I reply, trying to make a joke, but Ashley's not laughing.

"I hate this!" she says, then walks briskly away from me.

"Wait up!" I call after her, but she takes off her shoes and starts running down the hall. I chase after her, but it's like she's being pursued by a monster. She doesn't even wait for the elevator, taking the stairs to our room on the fourth floor of the hotel. By the time I catch her, she's crumpled by the door with her eyes shut tight like a steel trap.

"Do you have the key?" she asks.

I pull the key card from my small purse and put it into the door. "You okay?"

"I'm just tired and cold," she says. With the July night air outside still up in the 80s, the AC at the Traverse City Grand Hilton is running at the max.

"Ashley, I'm sorry about Carl," I say as we go into the room.

"It's not Carl," she says, crawling under the covers while still wearing all of her clothes. "It's all the Carls down there."

"I don't understand," I reply, sitting on the edge of my bed.

Ashley doesn't say anything as she shivers under the blankets.

"What can I do?" I ask, leaning over to touch the edge of her bed.

"Keep me warm," Ashley says. Her teeth are chattering like the sky is full of snow-filled clouds instead of summer stars. "I don't want to be cold again."

I'm not sure what she means, but she opens up the blankets and motions for me to crawl into bed with her. When I do, she holds me like someone free-falling from the sky.

I rub her arms to warm her up, but she keeps repeating how she's cold. Then we hear Mom and Carl crash into the room next door. Even through the thick wall, we can hear their yelling and what sounds like a chair getting turned over. There's more yelling, a door slam, and then the sound of the TV coming on loud. As all this is happening, Ashley starts shaking. I hold her tighter, clutching her like Mom held me when I was a sick child. When it seems like she's asleep, I crawl out of bed and grab my cell.

"Danielle, don't leave me alone," Ashley whispers softly. "Come back to bed."

"I was just going to call..."

She finishes my sentence, almost spitting out the word "Reid."

"I want you to meet him. Maybe you won't feel the same way if—"

Ashley cuts me off. "I don't want to meet him."

"But he's so cool. He's not a loser like Carl," I say, the words rushing out of me. "He's not immature like Evan. He's great-looking and he lov—"

Ashley cuts me off again, saying, "I know his type," although I don't believe her for one second.

"Why do you hate him so much?" I ask, wondering if the emotion of the evening coupled with the lateness of the hour will finally allow her to be honest with me.

"Because he's going to hurt you."

"But I love him," I say, not even stumbling over the word "love" this time.

"That's why he's going to hurt you." Ashley's sitting up in bed now.

"You don't understand," I say.

"Understand what?"

Even as the words leave my mouth, I want to pull them back in. "Being in love."

"You're still so naive, Danielle."

"Reid is just so special. It doesn't matter that he's older. It doesn't matter that—"

"Are you trying to justify this to me or to yourself?"

I don't answer, so Ashley says softly, "Look, Danny, I just want to protect you."

"I can protect myself."

"Who knows how many other girls Reid—"

"Ashley, stop talking that way."

"Fine, I'll stop talking because you don't want to listen anyway," Ashley announces. I try to restart the conversation, but if I mention Reid's name, it's like I'm pushing an off button.

I lie down on my bed with Ashley in the next bed, still huddled up under the covers. My head is spinning, probably more than even Carl's drunk skull. I feel like I'm back on the merry-go-round and all the faces in my life are whirling past me. Every time Reid's smile beams at me, I know I've finally figured out what I always wanted to know: love is real.

· · ·

"Where's Carl?" I ask Mom the next morning as she puts the coffee cup to her mouth with her right hand. With her left, she's fiddling with the pair of cheap sunglasses she's wearing.

"He's still asleep," she says, then she sets down the coffee cup, which is good because her hand is shaking. I feel like all these well-dressed people here in the hotel café are staring at us.

"Are you okay, Mom?" I ask. Ashley shifts in the seat next to me.

"Just tired," she replies, reaching into her purse. "Wasn't the wedding beautiful?"

"I guess," I say as I watch Mom pull out cigarettes and a lighter. This morning, I see the wedding in a darker light. On my wedding day, there'll be no Dad to give me away or have the first dance, like Brittney and her dad shared. There'll be no beautiful bridesmaids or grinning groomsmen. No flowers, no fancy hotel, no happy family pictures.

"Excuse me, you're not allowed to smoke in the restaurant," the waiter says, tapping my mother on the shoulder almost the second she lights up.

"What?"

"This is a no-smoking establishment," he says, crossing his arms while Mom inhales.

"Fine," my mother retorts, then puts out the cigarette in the fancy hotel coffee cup.

"It's no big deal," I say.

"Let's get Carl's lazy ass out of bed and get out of here," my mom says as she throws a few dollars on the table. Ashley looks like she wants to die as she follows my mom and me out of a room where we obviously shouldn't have been sitting in the first place.

• • •

"You ask him," Ashley whispers to me as soon as we drive away from the hotel.

"He's in a bad mood," I whisper back. As on the drive up, the front seat's full of music instead of conversation, while our backseat's full of whispers and deep sighs, mostly from Ashley. I feel bad, since I'd begged her to come with me so I wouldn't be trapped with just Mom and Carl. I owe her, yet again.

"Please, do this favor for me," Ashley says.

"Carl!" I yell over the booming greatest hits of heavy metal.

He doesn't answer; his eyes are focused on the road in front of him. My mother doesn't turn around, either. I can't tell what her eyes are focused on because those cheap sunglasses remain firmly on her head. "Carl!" I shout, this time with a short kick of the seat.

He turns down the music, sighs, and then yells back at me, "What do you want?"

"How far is Tawas from Traverse City?" I ask, as if trying to win a politeness award.

"You think I'm Rand F'n McNally or something?" is his less than helpful response.

"It's on the other side of the state, I think," Mom says, sounding confused.

"Why the hell do you care?" Carl snaps back. He sounds hungover.

"Don't talk to my daughter that way," Mom says to Carl.

There's silence in the car; it's the polar opposite of last night. Carl turns the music back up, but Ashley squeezes my hand, forcing me to press on.

"We'd like to go Tawas," I shout over the music.

"I need to get home," Carl says. I want Mom to correct him: our house isn't his home, and his desire to smack a softball with a bat is hardly a pressing need. But Mom lets it go, like a lot of stupid things he says or does.

Another squeeze from Ashley. "Please, this is important," I say, trying to sound pitiful.

Mom turns to face us. "What's going on? Ashley, do you know someone there?"

Ashley looks out the window, not at Mom, when she answers, "Nobody, we just used to vacation there, that's all."

Although I don't know why she wants to visit, I keep going. "Ashley says it's a really nice place and..."

Carl hurls himself back into the conversation. "Your friend isn't driving, I am," he says.

Mom smiles at me, then speaks to Carl. "Carl, as long as we're this far north..."

"It's at least four hours out of the way," Carl barks. "And besides, I don't want to get stranded over in hillbilly hell."

"Hillbilly hell?" Mom says.

"Yeah. Traverse City and the cities on Lake Michigan are nice, if you're rich like your stuck-up sister. But over on the Lake Huron side, especially around Tawas, it is nothing but hillbillies, inbreeds, and junkies!" Carl doesn't realize that he's shouting. "It's like Detroit, except with wasted white trash rather than crackheads."

"Take that back," Ashley whispers.

"What did you say?" I whisper back.

"Take it back," she says louder, clearly aiming at the front seat, but Carl's not responding.

"Ashley, let it go," I say, but her anger's growing. I've seen this side of her only a few times at school, mainly if someone's mean to me. If someone says the wrong thing at the wrong time, she can go from calm to storm in ten seconds flat.

"Take it back," Ashley repeats, leaning forward, then reaching her long arm into the front seat. She's pointing at Carl, but he's staring at the road in front, not the rage behind him.

"What the hell are you talking about?" Carl says, finally acknowledging Ashley.

"I said take it back," Ashley says, louder now.

"What is she talking about?" Carl asks Mom, who seems to be shrinking in her seat.

"Ashley, come on, it's not that important," I say, trying to protect her.

"Take it back! What you said about people there." Ashley kicks Carl's seat.

"Unless you want to walk back to Flint, I suggest you knock it off!" Carl shouts at her.

"Take it back," she repeats like a machine gun. "Take it back. Take it back. Take it back. Take it—"

"Mom," I yell, but she's lost behind her shades.

"I didn't realize your friend was such a nut job," Carl says, then laughs.

"For the last time, take it back," Ashley says.

Mom finally speaks. "Carl, for God's sake, just—"

"Shut up!" Carl shouts back. "Shut up, all of you. Are you all on the rag or what?"

Ashley springs from the backseat, but she doesn't reach for Carl. Instead she snatches the sunglasses off my mother's face. Mom turns around so fast she doesn't take the time to hide her blackened left eye.

"Take it back or I'll call the police," Ashley says, whipping out her cell phone.

"Ashley, there's no need," Mom says, embarrassed and ashamed.

Carl doesn't say anything, but pushes down hard on the brakes and pulls the car over to the shoulder. All of us lurch forward as the car stops. Carl looks hard at my mother, then turns to face Ashley. His eyes are hot with anger, but Ashley's are pure fire.

"Who do you think you are?" Carl asks.

Ashley doesn't say anything; time stands still in silence. She's looking at my mom's sunglasses, holding them up to the light, like a prism.

Carl looks like he wants to jump in the backseat and smack Ashley; instead, he hisses out his question again. "I said, who in the hell do you think you are?"

"Maybe I'm a piece of hillbilly white trash," Ashley says with no emotion whatsoever in her voice. "Or maybe I'm the person who is going to see you fucking rot in fucking jail if you ever fucking hit Danny's mother again! You understand that, you psycho asshole?"

With that, she hands the sunglasses back to my mother, then looks out the window.

"Take us home," Mom says softly. Carl looks like a pot ready to boil, but says nothing. I think Ashley scared him. She sure scared me. I've seen many sides of Ashley, but not this one. It's like a whole different person is hiding inside of her.

It takes us a while to get back to I-75 south. Once we're on the highway, Ashley whispers to me, "Thanks for asking."

"Thanks for sticking up for my mom," I say, feeling guilty that I didn't fill that role.

"Why does she put up with him?" Ashley whispers, but before I can answer, she sighs and says, "I know why. She loves him."

"I guess," I mutter. That word, those emotions, all jumbled up in my life.

"Love destroys everything," Ashley says, in a tone as dark as the July day is bright.

I ignore her strange statement. Instead, I just say, "I'm sorry."

"For what?" she asks.

"For my family," I say, realizing that includes Carl, hate it or not.

"Like I said. Love destroys everything."

"Well, I'm still sorry for all this."

"It's okay." There's that sadness in her eyes again, which seems older than her years.

She turns to look out the window, and stays that way for the rest of the trip, like she's in a trance. Her eyes are hidden from me, but there's a sound of sorrow coming from deep inside her.

I put my hand on her shoulder, then say, "It's okay, Ashley, we'll be home soon."

She doesn't turn around, but I hear her say, "Home isn't always where you think it is."

"God, Ashley, that is such a cliché." I tell her that a lot.

"Maybe," she mumbles. "But Danny, doesn't that mean it says something so profound and pure and hurtful that we soften the impact by calling it a cliché?"

I don't answer and she lets it go. As we drive, Ashley's deep in thought and so am I. She's right: home isn't where you think, because the heart takes you places you never imagined.

10

MONDAY, JULY 21

"**Have you ever seen anything** cooler than these?" Reid asks me, showing off another new pair of fancy sunglasses with slick silver frames, diamonds, and a brown tint.

Before I can say anything, Reid continues, "They're Gucci. Worth five fucking bills." We're driving over to his house. His mom's at work, and Reid wants some private time with me. Mom thinks I'm with Evan. That's because Ashley won't lie for me anymore, or rather, I won't ask her to lie for me. She stood up for me and my mom, so I can't ask anything more of her.

Reid told me that some of the girls who hang around his house are jealous of me, so I'm usually there before the party starts, like today. The way they glare at me, especially Angie, seems to be saying I'm not good enough for Reid––who now seems to be reading my mind.

"Hey, I told Tony that I didn't want Angie at my house any-more," Reid says as we turn down Jennings Road. He's driving, but I've got one hand on the wheel.

"Really?"

"I told him he had to choose: he could come over, but not with her," Reid boasts. "I told him that he'd be better off without that lying skank."

"Ouch," I say, then laugh.

"She's always spreading rumors about me that aren't true," he says.

My fingers move from the steering wheel to the side of his face. "Drama queen."

"That's why you're so cool, Danielle," he continues as we pull down his street. "You're so mature for your age."

I don't say anything; instead I kiss him on the side of his unshaven face. He doesn't turn for a full frontal kiss because we're both stunned to see Vic and Evan sitting together on the curb in front of Reid's house.

"You're not welcome here!" Reid shouts to Vic as he pulls into the driveway.

"We need to talk," Vic shouts back, moving toward the Viper.

"Danielle, this doesn't concern you," Reid says sharply, then points at the passenger door. No sooner do I get out than Vic gets in.

I walk to the curb where Evan's still sitting.

"What are you doing here?" I ask, sitting a few feet from him.

"I'd ask the same thing," Evan responds.

"You don't understand," I counter.

"I understand you've been telling your mom that you're spending time with me," Evan says, his voice cracking.

"What do you mean?"

"I called the other day for you."

"I told you not to do that."

"Well, I guess I'm not a puppy dog anymore who just does what he's told."

"Evan, it's not like that," I say, trying to force a smile.

"Yes, it is," Evan says. "You think you can do or say anything and I'll still like you."

"Wait, Evan, I—"

"And you know what? You're right. That's how much I care about you. That's how pathetic I am. No wonder you don't like me. It's not because I don't drive an expensive car, get stoned, or have cool friends. It's because I'm pathetic."

"Stop saying that," I say, trying to reassure him.

"Since we're only ever going to be friends, let me tell you something, as a friend. Let's walk away." Evan gets off the curb and starts down the street. I quickly light up a smoke and follow him, but don't speak. I guess I owe him my silence for his speech.

"Think about the people you've met at Reid's," Evan says, pointing toward Reid's house.

"What about them?"

"Is that who you want to be?" Evan asks.

I think about Becca, my closest friend at Reid's. "Sure," I reply. Who wouldn't want to live like Becca? I know she's not always reliable, but who is?

"You're better than that," Evan says, pointing at me. "You deserve better than that."

"No, I don't," I say, blowing out the smoke that makes Evan, but not me, cough.

"Look, I'm just saying," he starts, but the nicotine is my angry adrenaline fuel.

"You're saying you're better than these people," I snap.

"I am."

"You work at Halo flipping burgers and making fries. That's real cool," I shoot back.

"At least I work," he says. "You think Reid's friends have jobs?"

"They have jobs," I say, instinctively defending them. But I realize that while most of them have money, they do always seem available to hang out whenever Reid wants them around.

"Stealing shit and selling weed isn't a job," Evan says, walking back toward Reid's house. "How do you think your boyfriend gets his money?"

"I don't know."

"Just because you act grown-up," Evan says, "don't assume you are."

"You're not the boss of me!"

"It's a good thing, because if I was, I wouldn't let you hang out with those people. If I was your boyfriend," he whispers, "I'd treat you better than this."

"You don't know what you're talking about, Evan."

"Maybe I don't," he yells over his shoulder as he walks away. "But Vic does. Ask him how Reid gets his money."

"What do you mean?" I'm almost chasing him down the street. He must be laughing at the idea of my chasing him. When I catch up to him, he's standing next to his brother's junker car, looking almost as beaten up. "Evan, what's wrong with you?"

"I'm sorry. I just want more for you," he says softly. "I guess it's not my place."

I manage a smile, look at Reid's house, then mutter to myself, "But *this* is mine."

"I'm walking home. Would you tell Vic for me?" Evan asks. "Sure thing."

"And ask him what I told you, okay?" Evan adds.

My smile disappears as Evan walks down the street alone. Part of me wants to follow him, to comfort him, even to hug him. But my feet won't move toward him. Instead I go back and wait for Reid to return. It seems everybody, from Evan to Mom to Ashley, doesn't want me with Reid—but I can't imagine myself anymore without him. They don't know him and they can't see what I see.

"Where's Reid?" I ask two guys standing on the back porch. Reid's plan was to get me home before the party started, but Vic and Evan got in our way. Reid's still not back.

"He split, I think," one says, then offers me a hit on a joint. I don't recognize these guys, but a lot of people come and go at Reid's house.

"No, thanks," I say, starting to walk away.

"It's good shit," the other mutters.

"Whatever," I snap. I'm on edge, wondering if Reid will be mad I'm still here.

"Chill, bitch," the first one says, taking the hit I passed on.

"Why do you want to know?" the second guy asks.

"Yeah, who do you think you are?" the first one says into a cloud of smoke.

"I'm Reid's girlfriend," I announce, blow them a kiss, and walk away feeling higher than whatever they were smoking could make me. It's nice to have a label sometimes. I head inside. It's mostly the same crew, although every now and then I'll notice some new faces. They're still people I mostly don't know, and it's hard to learn much about them other than their favorite movies and video games. Everybody over here talks a lot, laughs a lot, but nobody really says anything that matters. Mostly they talk about how drunk they're going to get, how stoned they already are, or how they plan to get drunk or stoned tomorrow. No wonder they laugh so much.

I'm feeling tense, thinking about Evan and wondering if I'm busted with Mom. The temptation to get drunk or stoned has never been greater, but loyalty matters more. I've betrayed Ashley in so many ways this summer; not getting drunk or high is my shout-out to her. It's bad enough when Mom says, "I told you so," but it's worse when your best friend has that same look in her eye.

Reid finally passes through the house. Sometimes he acts

like I'm the center of his universe, but other times, like tonight, I'm just some comet passing through his sky. He mouths the words "Not now, I'm busy," but lifts his new shades to give me full eye contact before heading away. I guess if he was always available, then I'd never appreciate just how good it feels to have him by my side.

I wait around for another hour, but Reid's still nowhere in sight. I'm just getting ready to leave, when I bump into Becca, or rather she and her glassy eyes bump into me.

"Hey! It's Reid's girl," Becca says, then giggles. A stoner giggle.

"Do you know where he is?" I ask, since my own search proved futile.

"Not sure. Just follow the cute girls and that's where you'll find him," Becca says. Seeing the frown come over my face, she adds, "Don't worry, you're his main girl."

"I hope so," I mumble.

"You're so lucky," Becca says, motioning for me to hand her a smoke.

"What do you mean?" I respond. Luck isn't a word I use to describe my life.

"Reid is like so fucking *it*," she says, almost spitting on me with the "t" sound.

"It?"

"Well, I don't need to tell you he's hot," Becca says. "Hey, don't tell Wayne I said that. Wayne's jealous of Reid. Tony, Angie, all these people like Reid, but they're also jealous."

I just nod, and then hand Becca my last cigarette.

"Wayne wants to be Reid, just like Vic wanted to be Reid," she says before she lights up.

I want to ask about Vic, but mainly I want to hear more about Reid. I shut up, so she goes on.

"Reid's the coolest guy I know," she says through more stoned giggling.

"Not everybody thinks so." I don't list Evan or the rest of the anti-Reid club.

"They're haters," she says, then blows a smoke ring. "They hate him because they can't be him. There's only one Reid, but lots of haters."

"No haters here," I say, looking around the crowded room. "I guess that's why the party's always at Reid's house."

"The party's not at Reid's *house*, the party's wherever Reid *is*," Becca says.

"I just wish I could find him, then," I say, looking at my watch. "Curfew calls."

"Curfew?" she asks, letting out another giggle.

It's so embarrassing whenever I say things that remind people I'm not an adult.

"You need a ride?" Becca asks, but before I can respond, she yells, "Wayne!"

He shouts from halfway across the room, "What do you want?"

"Can we give . . . um, I'm sorry, what's your name?"

"Never mind," I mumble. "If you see Reid, tell him that Danielle had—"

"I knew that." She looks embarrassed. "Wayne, can we give Danielle a ride home?"

"Tell Reid that I have to leave," I say, then walk through the throng of party guests, but it's as if I'm invisible. I turn to look at Becca before I exit; she's still smoking my cigarette. That's all I am to her: a cloud of smoke. She's not my friend, she's just like everybody else here—just somebody I know. It's only Reid who understands me.

I get maybe fifty feet when I hear a rumbling sound. It's Vic's junker. He turns down the music, but the engine's almost as loud.

"Hey, you seen Evan?" he shouts.

"He walked home. Sorry, I was supposed to tell you," I shout back.

He pulls closer, then yells, "You wanna ride?"

"I'm cool," I yell back, and keep walking.

"Look, everything's cool," he shouts. "It's a long way to your house; climb in."

I get in and we talk about nothing for most the trip, until we pull into Circle Pines. My hands are almost shaking, and not just from the speed bumps.

"Vic, can I ask you something?" I finally manage to say.

He pulls the car to a stop near some empty trailers, which is easy to do. Every day I see people pack up and leave Circle Pines. They must be going someplace better; I can't imagine they could go anyplace much worse. The For Sale signs on most of the trailers have yellowed as they've made their way through winter, spring, and now summer.

"How long have you known Reid?" I ask.

"We went to high school together," he says. I notice he doesn't say they graduated together.

"What's going on with the two of you?"

He fiddles with the radio. "We have some history."

"You used to be friends, right?" I ask.

Vic just stares through his cracked windshield. "I don't think Reid has any real friends," he says.

I laugh louder than I should. Reid's right, Vic is an idiot. How his parents could produce one son as smart as Evan and one as dumb as Vic is beyond me. "All those people—"

"Listen, let me tell you about all those people at Reid's house," Vic says, trying to sound serious. "Those people are not friends. Friends are equals, but those people worship Reid, like I used to. They're not friends, they're followers. And because of that, it's only a matter of time."

"Until what?"

"Until they find their own way and leave him," Vic says. "Like I did."

"He kicked you out," I tell Vic.

"Is that what Reid told you?"

"Maybe," I say.

"Well, that's kind of true, I guess," Vic continues. "We had a falling out."

"Over what?"

"You don't want to know," he says, then pumps the gas pedal.

"Yes, I do," I mumble, not letting on that I'd already over-heard part of the story.

"Okay, let me help you understand Reid by acting like him," he says.

"What do you mean?"

"I'll do something for you if you do something for me," he says. "That's how Reid operates, you should know that by now."

I let the remark slide, but know I'll chew on it later. "What do you want?" I ask.

"Be nice to my brother."

"I am," I tell him, but we both know it's a lie.

"No, no, you're not. He likes you so much. Evan and I don't have much in common, or much to talk about. But he still talks about you all the time."

"But I don't—"

"I didn't say you have to fuck him," Vic says, then laughs. "Just don't fuck him over."

"Okay, Vic, I promise I'll be nicer to him," I say grudgingly. "Now it's your turn."

"First thing I remember us doing was in junior high. Reid and I collected money for that Jerry Lewis telethon," he starts. "Then we took all the money and spent it at McDonald's."

"You were kids," I say.

"Fine, here's some more recent history," he says. "I'd boost stuff from the place I worked, then give it to Reid. He'd sell it, and we'd split the cash. I'd work someplace, get caught and fired, then get a new job. At Best Buy I said I was done, but Reid called and I got back in. After I got caught, they said they'd press charges unless I returned the stuff. Now, I've done time before—"

"Really?"

"Reid didn't tell you that either?" Vic asks.

"No," I mutter.

"When Reid and I were sixteen, we were boosting cars for this chop shop guy that Reid knew over in Burton," Vic says. "We got busted. A short stint, and then a long probation if..."

"If you didn't do it again," I finish.

Vic laughs. "If we didn't get caught again."

"Oh."

"It was pretty cool, boosting cars," Vic says. It looks like he's trying not to smile.

"Wasn't it scary?"

"That was the cool part: the rush of doing it. It's all about the risk. Rich people ski and skydive, but we'd boost cars— especially rich people's cars. One time, we got this Hummer."

"A Hummer. That must have been sweet."

"That was the coolest part, Danielle. After you boosted the car, before you dropped it or chopped it, you'd be riding around thinking, 'This is my car, this is my life.' It was like playing with toy Matchbox cars, except we were using the real thing." There was more fondness than regret in his voice.

"But you're done, right?" I ask him.

"I'm done playing pretend. All I need is to boost one last

sweet ride, then get out of Flint. I could change the paper and plates, or maybe get it chopped for a couple of stacks."

"What if you got caught?"

"Sometimes, I wish I would," Vic says.

"You don't think prison would be bad?" I ask in shock.

"I'm living in my parents' basement trying to avoid getting high most days. I've got no education, no job, and most of my friends are shallow stoners I know from Reid's, so I got nothing there. Maybe I *should* go back to boosting wheels."

"So you don't steal cars anymore?"

"We switched up a while back, started doing electronics. It was easier to boost, easier to hide, and to sell," Vic says. "Never let it be said that we didn't do things the easy way."

"So what happened with Best Buy?"

"I told Reid I needed the stuff back, but he blew me off," Vic says. He sounds more sad than angry. "He knows I won't turn him in. All thieves can do is steal or squeal on each other."

"So what were you doing there tonight?" I ask.

"I told Reid that I'm done with this life. And this life means him. I'm getting out."

"Of Flint?"

"Not just out of Flint, but away from my family," he says with a sigh.

"I know that feeling," I say.

"No, it's not like that. That's how you think when you're like you, just a kid. That's how I've been thinking, like a kid, but I'm done with all that. I don't want to stay around and have

Evan watch his older brother fuck things up all the time. I'm his big brother; I'm supposed to be setting an example. For me, this life is through."

"I don't believe you," I tell him, with all of Mom's similar promises, all broken, ringing in my ears.

"You don't *have* to believe me about Reid, or anything I said. But what's that saying, actions speak louder than words? Well, you just watch." He sounds like he's trying to talk himself into something. "All I need is some new wheels to replace this junker. Once I get 'em I'll be a thousand miles away. Evan won't be embarrassed by his loser brother anymore."

"He doesn't say that about you," I say, strangely lying for Evan. I guess I've already started keeping my part of the promise: I'm being nice to him.

"Doesn't matter, I'm done," Vic says. "How much longer would it last?"

"What do you mean?"

"I've been doing this for years: getting high, taking jobs, stealing stuff, getting fired, getting another job," Vic says. "I've been going to Reid's house since you were in junior high."

There's not a cloud in the sky, but lightning hits. "I knew you were one of the guys there that one night. You knew I'd come on to him when I was drunk."

"After I heard about that and how upset you were, I told Reid that he should apologize, but he just blanked me out," Vic says. "But hey, you're over it now and it's all worked out."

"What do you mean?"

"Look, you ended up with Reid, so you're happy and it doesn't matter if everybody but you can see how wrong he is," Vic says, putting the car into drive.

"You and your brother, you're both just jealous," I shoot back at him.

"Maybe, I don't know. If I come back in five years and head over to Reid's, if he's not in prison, you know what'll be different at that house on Jennings Road?"

"What?"

"Nothing," Vic says as we start driving again toward my house. "It'll be the same people, the same bullshit. Everybody's getting older, but nobody's growing up. All those people, they're like me: they've dropped out of school, and they've dropped out of life. They think they're free, but they just don't see the bars on the cage, like I do now. Danielle, is that what you want to be doing five years from now, the exact same thing with the same people?"

I can't answer that, so I don't.

"I just need to get lucky, for once. People like Reid, they get all the luck. They got good looks and everything that comes with that. Me, my brother, other people, we didn't get that luck. Reid got blessed by some magic wand, while I got smacked in the face. I'm tired of it. You understand what I'm saying?" Vic's way too emotional.

The car stops, and so does my ability to speak.

"It's like this song I heard on an oldies station once," Vic says.

"What song?" I punctuate my question by slamming the rusty door behind me.

"It's by Tom Petty," Vic says. "I think it's called 'Even the Losers Get Lucky Sometimes.'"

11

FRIDAY, JULY 25

"Is Ashley there?" I ask, trying to stifle a yawn.

"Good morning from the Great White North, Danielle, eh!" Ashley's father says, trying to sound Canadian. "What's that about, eh? Everybody's loony up here, eh!"

"Can you tell her I called?"

"It would be more efficient to tell her when you don't call, eh!" He's trying to be funny, but he's being kinda mean. I've called Ashley every day she's been on vacation with her parents in Canada, and this is the last day. They've cut off her cell phone—same as my mother will do to me the second she checks my minutes—so I'm calling her at the hotel in Toronto.

"Sorry," I mumble.

"I was just kidding, Danielle. Ashley is lucky to have a friend like you," he says, dropping the attitude and the accent.

"Thanks," I mumble again, wondering if she'll feel the same when she comes home tomorrow and discovers that the conspiracy that she hatched with Vic and Evan to get me to break up with Reid didn't work. Every time they push me, I just pull closer to Reid.

"She's just finishing in the shower."

Then comes the awkward pause. A long awkward pause.

"So, is Toronto as much fun as Tawas?" I ask, desperate to break the silence.

"Tawas?"

"Ashley said you used to vacation there and—"

Before I can finish, he cuts me off. "Who told you that?"

"She did," I respond, but I can tell he's not listening. I struggle to hear the muted conversation my comment inspired.

"Danielle, just a moment." It's her mother now. "Ashley will be—"

"Did I say something wrong?"

More silence. Not awkward, but agonizing—which turns into endless.

"Hey, BFF," Ashley finally says.

"Hey, Ash," I say. "That was so weird, I asked your parents about Tawas, and—"

"How's Reid?" she asks, much to my surprise. But before I can answer, she says, "Let me guess, he's perfect."

"Ashley," I say, "I don't know where to start," and then the words rush out of me like water from a broken dam. I tell her that what other people think of Reid doesn't matter, all that matters is the time he and I spend together. The monologue ends with this: "It's like I was just waiting for my life to begin."

She sighs from a thousand miles away. "Oh, sweet young naive Danielle."

"Oh, wise Wizard of the Great North." I tease her right back.

"All of that is half a world away," Ashley announces.

"What do you mean?"

"Yesterday we went to the CN Tower and looked out over the city. There's millions of people here from all over the world. The drama of Flint seems very distant."

"I guess," I mumble.

"That's what everybody needs in their life, a high tower so they can see their life from afar. Then they'd know the things that are really important."

"Like?" I ask. But she doesn't answer. We're trapped in our thoughts, which can't bounce off of satellites. After another pause, she tells me about her trip, the shows they've seen, stuff they've done, and she says she'll tell me more when she gets home tomorrow. We say our last long-distance goodbye. Even though I love every second with Reid, I can't stop feeling angry at Ashley's perfect parents and perfect life. Like Vic said, some people are born lucky, and others of us find luck where we can.

• • •

"Danielle, you awake?" It takes me a moment to place the voice. It's Carl's, and his bald head is sticking into my room. I must've fallen back asleep after hanging up with Ashley.

"What do you want?" I ask, pulling the covers tight around me.

"I need to say something," Carl says, very slowly. I can't tell if he's hungover or just having a hard time speaking. Hangovers come easily to Carl; conversations between us do not.

"What?" I ask, but he's looking at the floor, not at me.

"I'll be at the table," he mutters, then shuts the door behind him.

I quickly get dressed, not because I want to see Carl, but because Reid and I are going driving again later today. Sometimes I wonder what would happen if Mom caught me, but most times, I just don't care what she thinks. I fix my hair and then drag myself out to talk to Carl.

He's sitting at the kitchen table, drinking coffee and smoking. When I got home last night, just seconds before curfew, he was on the sofa, drinking beer and smoking. Carl doesn't change, only his beverage does.

"Sit down," he mumbles. I walk slowly toward the table, unsure what's going on. For most of this summer, Carl and I have wanted the same thing: to leave each other alone. We share my mom's attention, an occasional meal, and this cramped crappy trailer, but nothing else.

"I'll stand," I say, then walk past him to get some juice from the fridge.

"Your mom wants me to apologize," Carl starts, and for once I'm interested in his words. If he's going to apologize, I'd better sit down, although I'll be near the edge of my seat wondering which of his many sins he wants to say he's sorry for first.

"For what?"

"For that thing in the car with your friend." He's speaking to the table in front of him, not to me. "Your mother said I was wrong to go off on her like that. You'll tell her, okay?"

I sip the juice, letting the coolness trickle down my sore

throat, from which no words will come. Carl's only apologizing because Mom wants him to; I guess since I won't be the obedient daughter anymore, she needs somebody else to boss around. Carl's not the bully, Mom is.

"Okay," I finally say, not so much to accept the apology but to break the silence. Carl grunts and I turn toward my room.

"I'm doing the best I can," I hear him mumble, almost like he doesn't really want me to hear what he's saying, maybe because he knows I can't believe him. If drinking, hitting my mom, and not working are the best he can offer, what's the worst?

"The best I can," Carl repeats, the words drifting toward me on smoke clouds. I know he's begging for acceptance in his own pathetic way, but even in the silence between us, I still hear faint echoes of his hand bouncing off Mom's face.

"Whatever, Carl," I say in a tone that smacks like the back of my own angry hand. I can't give in to this overture, so not only won't I accept it, I'll dramatically reject it. I head toward the bathroom, but the door's locked. After a few seconds, Mom emerges.

"You talk to her?" she asks Carl. Her hair is wet and in need of a new dye job.

"I tried," Carl mumbles, looking away from me. "In one ear and out the other."

"I'm going down to the pool to read," I announce.

"Don't you mean go meet your boyfriend?" Mom says. She puts on a robe and comes out to the kitchen table, quickly lighting up a smoke. "It's time for us to have a talk."

"A family talk?" I say, waiting for Mom to nod, which she does, so I can add, "I guess that means you can leave, Carl."

"That's enough of that," Mom says, but the message gets through. Carl puts out his smoke, then heads outside to do whatever it is he does to pass his day. Once the door closes, Mom sits at the table and asks the question I've been dreading. "When can I meet him?"

"Who?" I knew it was only a matter of time before Mom confronted me about where I was spending my days. I've run out of lies and excuses; she's run out of patience.

"This boy you're really spending time with," she says. "I know it's not Evan."

"You won't like him," I tell her. I've been avoiding home not just so I can spend as much time with Reid as he can spare, but also to avoid this conversation with my mother. "But it doesn't matter if you like him or not, because I do."

"Thank God you didn't say you loved him," she says, then sighs. I wanted to tell her that very thing, but I just knew this would be her reaction. My mom's so boring and predictable; no wonder I'd rather spend time with Reid.

"Why do you even care?" I say. She points toward a chair and I obey.

"What's his name? What grade is he in? Does he go to Carmen?" Mom asks. I find myself wishing Carl were here to throw me some slow softball pitches; Mom's tossing high hard ones. I duck her scorn by telling her little lies, figuring she'd rather hear those than the whole truth.

"He's going to be a senior, so he's just one year older." I'm trying to talk normal, trying to hide my deceit and the five-year difference between Reid and me. Maybe because I've never lied much to Mom before—I didn't have much of anything to lie about—she doesn't know what my truthless tone sounds like. "He's really nice and drives a really cool car."

"I worry about you so," my mom says.

"Why's that?"

She makes a half-grunt, half-laugh sound. "That's what I told my mom about your dad."

I bite my bottom lip, but don't say anything.

"When I gave you permission to date, I thought it was going to be with that nice boy Evan," she says, then adds yet another sigh.

"You thought wrong," I say sharply, wanting to ask her what she knows about nice boys.

"Lose that tone," she snaps back.

"Sorry," I say, but what my mother thinks is just not important anymore.

"Carl has a softball game tonight, and I'm not working," she says. "We'll all go to dinner together beforehand so I can get to know this boy who is taking so much of my daughter's time."

"I don't want to," I counter. "Watching Carl play softball belongs in the *Guinness Book of World Records* for most boring event in history."

Mom's tongue turns sharp. "I'm not asking you, I'm telling you."

"No."

"What did you say?" she says, pretending she didn't hear me, or maybe giving me another chance.

"I said no, I'm not going to see Carl's stupid softball game or have dinner with you two."

"Danielle, you're my daughter, you don't get to say no," she replies.

"Maybe you should learn how to say no yourself," I shoot back.

"What does that mean?" she says.

"You know what it means," I say, but I'm not angry with Mom; I'm feeling sorry for her. I want to save her from the ticking Carl time bomb.

"I said, lose that tone." She can't correct me on the facts, so she goes after the delivery.

"You lose Carl and I'll tell you what you want to know," I tell her, thinking about all the different things Reid's taught me. Now I can drive a car and a hard bargain.

"When did you get to be such a smart-ass?" is her non-response.

"When did you stop standing up for yourself?" I act on my words by standing up, leaving her behind, and slamming my bedroom door so hard that our trailer shakes.

• • •

As soon as Mom leaves for work, I call Reid. He tells me that Wayne and Becca are over, and I should get myself there. He doesn't offer to pick me up, so I'm back on my bike. But after arriving, I slide behind the wheel, not of a real car, but one in a video game.

"Ready to race again?" Reid asks. He's beaten me four times in a row; I don't expect number five to be any different. "There ain't nobody that can beat me at this or any game!"

"Bring it!" I shout, and we start another race. We're racing on the big screen at speeds up to two hundred miles per hour; I'm racing inside at about twice that speed. At the start of the summer, my days were spent sitting in my room, talking on the phone with Ashley, reading books, and riding my bike. A month later, I'm in Reid's basement room with his cool friends talking, laughing, and becoming a Race Car Hero.

"I own you!" Reid shouts as he passes me repeatedly. "Bow to the master."

"You just wait," I shout back.

"Is that a promise or a threat?" he cracks, then throws a hip in my direction.

"Both!" I tell him, bumping him back as our cars on the screen also crash into each other.

The fifth game finishes like all the others: with Reid in the winner's circle, leading him to sing out, "I'm the champion."

Wayne starts pouring a beer over Reid's head. Reid laughs, snatches the bottle from Wayne, shakes up the beer, then lets it loose on me.

"That's cold!" I shout, trying to cover up.

"That's the idea," Reid says, slapping fists with Wayne. "Better get out of those wet clothes."

"Very funny." I shoot him a mock pout, followed by a smile.

But Reid just stares and repeats, "I said, you'd better get out of those wet clothes."

"Reid, come on, cool it," Becca cuts in.

I'm looking at Becca, my eyes asking for more help, but she turns away.

"I was just busting you," Reid says, breaking the stare with a kiss as he pulls me closer to him. "Here comes my girl."

"Okay," I whisper.

"I'll get my own show later," he whispers, then kisses my neck.

"Reid, are we getting baked or what?" Wayne says, taking the first hit off a joint.

"Hell yes," Reid says. He sits down and pulls me onto his lap. Wayne's on the sofa and Becca's sitting on the floor, the back of her head resting between Wayne's legs.

"Danielle, this is good shit, you're sure?" Wayne says, offering me the joint.

"I'm good," I say, then reach for one of the open beers. I don't know how Carl can drink six or seven of these in a night when I can barely manage one; they taste so foul.

"Come on, this is some of our best stuff," Wayne says, then he takes a hit.

"Be cool, Wayne," Reid says.

"I am, she's not," Wayne mutters.

"What did you say?" Reid says.

"I'm sorry, Reid," Wayne says, earning a knee kiss from Becca. "Sorry, girl."

"She can do whatever she wants to do, isn't that right?" Reid says, taking the joint from Wayne. He gives me a big kiss before taking his extra-long house-rules hit.

Wayne just grunts, then stumbles over to the stereo, cranking up the sounds of 105FM, Flint's best radio station. I feel like I'm outside in the July heat: everything's hazy, and it's not just a contact high or the buzz from my one beer. The past month with Reid has been more like a dream than my waking life. Like the characters in Narnia or another fantasy world, I've walked into a strange land I never imagined.

There's no sense in letting Mom meet Reid because she won't be able to understand something that I can barely make sense of myself. You can't put love into words. I guess that's why poets, painters, and songwriters are always suffering, they're all trying to explain the unexplainable secrets of the human heart.

"Reid, do you have a camera?" I ask, which makes everybody laugh.

"A few of them," Reid says, then he and Wayne high-five. "Why?"

"I want some pictures of us, that's all," I reply. This sends Becca into action. She pulls her bright red cell out of her purse and snaps a quick photo of me with it. Reid kisses me on the lips, and Becca captures that moment as well. Everybody's laughing as we take turns snapping pictures. I linger on the photo that Reid takes of the four of us, our heads together like some multi-headed mythical beast, then think back to the wedding in Traverse City. I think of all the happy pictures of Brittney, her new husband, and his happy family, and how glad I am that there are no pictures of my mom's bruised face from the morning after. When your own family's let you down, your friends become your family.

12

SATURDAY, JULY 26

"**Danielle, what are you doing** driving?" Ashley asks as she walks over to the Viper.

"Cool, huh?" I say, then motion for her to get in the car. Reid's up front with me. He only let me drive the Viper into Ashley's driveway, but it was still a huge thrill.

"I guess," she says. She sounds about as unexcited as Reid was when I suggested this get-together. He said he really didn't want to meet Ashley, but with the summer halfway over, I had to show her not only that I could drive, but that I could drive the coolest car around.

"Welcome back," I say as I get out of the car to give her a big missing-you hug. We'd talked on the phone a lot, more than Mom wanted and less than Ashley desired. About the only people I can please anymore are Reid and my cell phone company's billing department.

"I brought you some stuff from Toronto," she says, returning the hug but sounding distracted. "Maybe tonight we could—"

"I'm a driving machine," I announce. "Come on, climb in, and let me show you."

"I don't know," Ashley says, very tentatively.

"I'm driving," Reid says, then gets out of the car. "She can't handle my six hundred horses."

I take a deep breath and hope for the best. "Reid, this is Ashley."

"Your BFF Ashley," she corrects me, poking me gently as she says it.

"What does that mean?" he asks.

"Best friends forever," we both say at the same time.

"Oh, I forget, your friend is still in high school," Reid says to Ashley.

"Are you from the Matrix?" Ashley asks, pointing to Reid's sunglasses. "Nice shades."

I snatch the glasses from Reid's face, then put them on. "Don't I look like a star?"

"You wanna buy a pair?" Reid asks Ashley, his now-naked green eyes looking annoyed.

"No, thanks," she replies, staring back at him. "Nice to meet you too."

"He's just kidding, Ash," I reassure her, but her response is just to keep staring at Reid.

"I know, it's okay," she says, but I don't believe her. Nor do I believe it when she reaches her hand out toward him. Reid looks skeptical, even confused at the gesture.

"It's cool," he says, throwing out a fist rather than an open hand.

Now Ashley looks confused. It's like two strangers in a foreign country speaking different languages. She looks over at me, then seems to stare right through Reid as she taps her fist lightly against his. She finally takes her eyes off him to inspect the two-seat Viper. Then she asks, "So where do I sit?"

"On my lap, I guess," I say with a laugh, although Ashley doesn't even crack a smile.

"Well, at least it's not the backseat," she says.

Reid puts the top up. I crawl in the passenger seat and Ashley climbs on top. Reid seems amused, but we don't talk about it. Instead, we listen to music that Reid chooses (T-Pain), and drive down I-75 at our usual eighty miles an hour. Once we get to the library and the car stops, Ashley bolts. I hand Reid back his glasses, then lean over to kiss him, but he turns away.

"You angry at me?" I whisper, my eyes looking away.

"Sure you don't wanna have fun instead of doing this?" Reid whispers in response.

"Maybe tonight at your house, but I need to see Ashley now." I wish Ashley could hear me saying this.

"Things are getting crazy, so I'm cooling things down for a while all around," Reid says.

"Just us?" I look up at him. Sometimes, like now, he seems so much taller than me.

"Nah, gotta cool it altogether," he says. I see Ashley outside the car, still staring at Reid.

"I understand," I say. Just a little white lie between lovers.

"So maybe next week sometime, if you wanna come over then," he says, putting on his shades. I kiss him, then wave goodbye and join Ashley at the library's front door. People all over the library must be looking up from their books and computers as Reid noisily peels out.

"Did you read the book this time?" Ashley asks, half-joking.

"The back of it," I confess.

She rolls her eyes, then laughs. "Well, I'm sure you're good at faking it."

"Ouch," I say. She pinches my arm and I pinch her back as we walk into the library.

The book discussion goes pretty well: Dave, Lauren and her friends, and this new girl Sarah Michelle talk the most. Sarah's pretty funny, or at least Ashley thought so, laughing at most everything she said. She's smarter than most pretty girls and prettier than most smart girls, although that kind of stuff doesn't bother me anymore.

"Let's see if Sarah wants to hang out with us. Is that okay?" Ashley says.

"I guess," I mumble.

"What's wrong?" She reads me better than any book.

"Can I just have a smoke first?" I say. Ashley rolls her eyes, just like old times. I head outside, while she finds Sarah.

I stand behind the library smoking and checking my cell phone messages. I call Reid, but he doesn't pick up. I think about calling Evan, but that would be the opposite of what Vic wants. Evan won't be happy unless I'm his girlfriend. I can't call any of the folks from Reid's. I don't know most of their names, let alone their phone numbers. I think about Vic asking me to imagine five years from now. Would I be like Wayne, Becca, and the rest hanging around Reid's: not moving forward, just swaying in the wind?

"You ready?" Ashley shouts from the front door.

"Where's Sarah?" I shout back as she walks over toward me.

"She's not coming," Ashley grumbles, sounding angry, hurt, rejected.

"Why not?" I ask, putting out the smoke on the concrete wall of the library.

"Guess everybody has a boyfriend they'd rather be with."

"You could have a boyfriend in an instant," I remind her. "Evan's so available."

"Shut up," she exclaims with great exaggeration.

"I know he likes you too," I say, trying to be nice, but instead I'm met with a hard glare. Ashley's eyes are darker now, thanks to the thick goth-like eye makeup she's applied.

"What, so I get your rejects?" she says, hands on her hips. "I'm not good enough."

"I was trying to be nice," I explain, expecting a shoulder pat, but her dark stare beams back at me like a laser.

"About time," she mumbles, then walks away. I catch up with her at the reflecting pool.

"What does that mean?" I ask as I sit down next to her.

"You haven't been real nice to me this summer," Ashley says, taking off her shoes.

"I'm sorry," I say, knowing I've been in the wrong and no words can make it right.

"I can't stay mad at you," she says, then puts her feet into the pool.

"Me either," I say, even though I'm not really mad at Ashley, just at myself.

She points toward my shoes. I kick them off, then plunge my feet into the cooling water. "This is nice," she says, then splashes a little water my way.

"What I said about Evan was just me trying to be nice about you getting a boyfriend."

"Really?"

"I think he would be your boyfriend, if you wanted one," I say.

"You just don't want to feel guilty," she says, splashing me again.

"Okay, you got me, that's part of it, but—"

"Guilt kills," Ashley announces in her best oracle tone.

"But still, I know he likes you and—"

"And love ruins everything," Ashley says. She's on a truth-telling roll.

"Ashley, don't talk that way." I splash her, but get nothing in return. She sits for the longest time looking at her reflection in the pool. The wind's pushing the water around, making both of our faces look distorted, like some crazy Halloween mask or funhouse mirror.

Finally she glares over at me and says, "If you love someone, they will leave you, and when they leave you, then you have nothing left except guilt and memories."

"Ash, I don't understand why you get this way."

"This summer, you've abandoned me. I don't need that again."

"Ashley, I won't do that."

"Yes, you will," she says with no emotion in her voice. "People always leave me."

I turn to face her, then hug her as I say, "I won't do that. We're best friends, forever."

"Forever doesn't last as long as you think," she says, back in her oracle mode again.

"What is wrong with you!" I ask in a begging tone, but I don't know if she hears me. She pulls her feet out of the pool like someone dropped in a live wire. I sit looking at my reflection. Not liking what I see, I start kicking wildly, and the water splashes all around me.

"There's something I want to say to you," Ashley says. "I thought about it the entire time I was away."

"What is it?"

She puts her hand on my shoulder and her face against mine and whispers, "You know, Danielle, 'best friends forever' isn't just an expression, it's a promise."

13

SUNDAY, AUGUST 3

"What class should I take first?" Mom asks. She's sitting at the table still dressed in church clothes. She's smoking, drinking black coffee, and looking at a Baker College catalog.

"I don't know," I say impatiently. We did church this morning and are talking about college this afternoon, but there's still plenty of beer around. Well, two out of three ain't bad.

"A little support would be nice," she says. "Matter of fact, you could use some support yourself. You're not to dress that way for church again."

"Whatever, Mom," I snap. Maybe a low-cut beater wasn't right for Sunday morning, but since I can't see Reid right now, I'll wear the gifts he's given me.

"Did you hear that sermon today?" she asks, then points for me to sit down with her.

"Maybe," I say. Truth is, I kinda slept through most of church. Actually, it was more like I was in one of those Ashley-style trances where I block everything else out. When she does that, I never know what she's thinking, but my thoughts are always drawn to Reid.

Mom takes a puff, then says, "It was about being truthful."

"So?" is my eye-hiding response.

"I want to know all about this boy you are dating, now."

"I told you before, it's none of your business."

"If it involves you, baby, it *is* my business," is her expected response.

I try to get up from the table, but she actually grabs my hand. She glances quickly at the set of silver skull rings I'm now wearing, then sighs. Like my new clothes, the rings are gifts from Reid. I try to shake my hand free, but she holds on tight as I say, "Mom, you just wouldn't understand because—"

"Because I'm not fifteen and immature." She blows smoke in the air, but it feels like it's in my face.

"No, because my boyfriend is nice to me, treats me like I'm somebody special, and tells me I'm beautiful. He's got a cool car and not some crappy truck. Oh, yeah, did I mention he's a good-looking guy who isn't a drunk! Unlike some people." I point toward the bedroom, where Carl is, of course, sleeping off a hangover.

"That's quite enough of that."

"I wish *you'd* had enough of that loser," I snap back.

"I said enough!" She slaps the table with her right hand so hard that drops of black coffee explode out of the white cup. The sound stuns us both, but it allows me to get my hand free from hers. "You've got no right to say those things about Carl."

"I never said Carl's name."

"You're developing quite the attitude, young lady."

"Oh, I also forgot to mention my boyfriend doesn't hit me."

"That's not your business!" she shouts, then adds, "Nor, for that matter, is it Ashley's."

"Well, somebody—," I start, but then figure, why bother! I'd rather spend my time trying to figure out why Ashley reacted the way she did than talking to my deaf, dumb, and blind mother.

"Look, I want some answers," Mom says.

"So do I," I say. "How can you let men treat you like they do?"

As I hoped, that question silences her. Her eyes flash anger as her shaking hand grinds the remains of her cigarette into an overstuffed ashtray. I shake my head, no longer in disgust but with sadness, and then walk slowly back to my room. Mom doesn't say anything to me; instead she tosses the Baker College catalog into the trash, like so many wasted dreams.

. . .

I grab my bike and head out to Fenton Lawn to smoke and swing. I need to work out some of this energy, and try to relax. After these fights with Mom, I've got to talk to someone. I try Ashley but she doesn't pick up. I can't call Evan because I'm angry at him for not lying for me, so I decide to call Reid. Not to discuss Mom—I'm sure that kind of talk would remind him I'm still a stupid fifteen-year-old—but just to hear his voice and picture his face in my mind.

He doesn't pick up his cell, which is becoming all too familiar because of how busy he is, although he always calls back. I know he said we needed to cool things for a while, but I'm so upset that normal rules can't apply. I hate to act all needy, but I really have to talk with him, so I try his house phone. It's been a long time since I dialed the Barkers' number, so I hope it's right.

"Hello," a familiar female voice answers.

"Um, is Reid there?" I ask.

"Danielle?"

I know who this is. "Yeah. Is that Kate?"

"Hey, what's up?" she asks.

"What are you doing there?" I ask quickly.

"My dad dropped me off for the day. It's my mom's birthday," Kate says.

"I didn't know," is all I can think to say.

There's a long pause. Since Kate and I haven't talked in years, I'm not surprised we don't fall right back into best-friend rhythm. We somehow kick-start the conversation, talking about nothing but her summer, her boyfriend, her tan, always about *her*. When she's run out of things to brag about, I get back to my business. "So, is Reid there?"

"So, you called for Reid?" she asks, but her tone shows she knows about us. I don't know why, but part of me didn't want her to find out, while another part—especially after her brag-fest—embraces this sweet and spiteful moment.

"Well, he and I have—," I start slowly, not sure how much Reid would want me to say.

"So, my former best friend is blowing my brother," she says, then laughs.

I hate that word, but I don't contradict her. Mom just reminded me that it's wrong to lie.

"Kind of surprises me, though," she says, with another small laugh.

I know it's a trap, but I can't resist. "Why's that?"

"He's not into butter faces," she says, very softly, like a gun with a silencer.

"What do you mean?"

"That's what Reid calls girls like you," she continues. "Butter faces. You know, everything's hot *but her face.* You finally got some great boobs, Danielle, but—"

"I don't believe you," I snap, even as I'm melting like a butter face inside. Did Reid really say this about me, or is she lying? I can't ask because I don't really want to know.

"That's a mistake, old BFF," Kate says. "Why would I lie to you?"

"To hurt me," I say, almost embarrassed to admit that I can be hurt.

"Danielle, why would I want to hurt you?" she counters. "Look, we were best friends and we let some stupid shit happen between us. I know we're different now, but girl, I don't want to see you heartbroken and all that shit."

"Really?" I'm trying to say as little as possible to cover up my pre-cry sniffling.

"Really," Kate says. "Believe me, my brother is going to hurt you."

"No, he—" But I pause.

"I know he says he needs you. He tells you you're hot. He gives you shit."

I don't say anything as Kate tells me about my life.

"Better I tell you than you learn it the hard way, but Reid doesn't give a shit about you," she continues as I hold back those tears. "Reid cares about Reid—or can't you see that?"

"No, you're wrong."

"He's got you tangled up in his bullshit," she says. "You boosting shit for him yet?"

"No," I snap back, troubled mostly by the word "yet."

"Just wait, it's part of his game," she says.

"You're wrong, you don't know him at all," I counter.

"He's my fucking brother, Danielle!" she shouts. "I know what he is."

"Lay off him! You know better than anyone what a hard life Reid's had." I'm shouting now as I decide to fight back and stand up for Reid, as he did for me that day in his basement.

"Hard life?" Kate laughs.

"He told me how your dad hit and burned him. How your mom's drunk all the time."

"God, he's fed you a whole line of bullshit," she says. "You believe that shit?"

"It's true."

"Mom's never been drunk that I know of," she says without any giveaway wavering in her voice. "Dad never hit or burned anyone. Reid did that himself; he's a burner."

"What?"

"That's why my parents live apart," she continues. "Dad wanted to ship Reid to a boot camp to get his shit together, but Mom wouldn't have it. They fought all the time, and finally it was too much and Dad left. Reid burned more than himself: he burned down our family."

"Why are you lying to me?"

"Danielle, I'm not the one who's lying," Kate says, and then says nothing else. My vocal cords are silent but my nose, eyes, and throat create a symphony of stifled crying sounds.

"Are you there?" Kate says after a few minutes.

I clear my throat, then say defiantly before I hang up, "Just tell Reid I called."

. . .

Just like the night I called 911, I'm on my bike again pedaling furiously, rain pouring down my face. But this time the rain is my own tears. It's a monsoon of emotion. By the time I get home, Carl's gone to Sunday softball; Mom's doing her two-to-ten waitress shift. I call Reid one last time and, through a tornado of tears, leave a message begging him to come save me—then I collapse on my bed. All I want to do is sleep, then wake up, not in a few hours, but back at the start of this morning. Then maybe I could avoid the fight with my mom and the spite of Kate's lies. Or maybe I could wake up before I met Reid. Wake up back in my boring, simple life again.

The honking of the Viper's horn and the pounding bass

wake me. I look at the clock and see it's a few minutes past seven. Reid's come to save me, so I pull myself together. I do a quick makeup job, run a brush through my hair, and put on another tight tank top Reid gave me.

I lock the door behind me, and the heat that's been building all day hits me. I've had nothing to eat since breakfast, so I'm feeling sick, with a stomach full of salty tears. Before I can join Reid in the Viper, I need to sit down. The top's up and the music's blasting, but with the tinted windows, I can't see him. He's waiting inside while I'm wavering, sitting on the short three-step porch. It's like all of Kate's lying and Mom's hating has crippled me. I'm broiling in the August sun waiting for Reid to come to me. I tell myself that when he does, everything will be okay.

The music grows louder. Reid's head appears from out of the Viper. His shirt's off, his sunglasses are on, and he's got a red towel around his neck. Snapping his Razr phone shut, Reid throws the towel at me as he shouts, "Climb in! It's time for night swimming!"

I take a deep breath, stand up, and turn to go back inside for my bathing suit. Not that ugly black one-piece, but a hot red bikini Reid and I bought together.

"Where you going?" he asks, but before I can answer, or unlock the door, he says, "Baby, you don't need anything but your sexy self."

Kate's wrong. I'm not a butter face, I'm Reid's baby.

On the way out to the lake, we don't talk a lot. I'm afraid if I start talking that I'll somehow blow it by mentioning one of

Kate's petty little lies. We stop, grab some fast food, take the Viper through one of those deluxe car washes, and then keep driving. I notice we're not headed toward one of the Chain of Lakes or any of the places we've gone swimming in the past. We pull onto a dirt road marked by No Trespassing signs. Reid blows by it. He's driving slower than usual, probably so the dust from the road doesn't mess up the fresh wax.

He parks near a fence with another No Trespassing sign, then says, "This is the place."

"Where are we?" I ask.

As he puts his sunglasses on the dash, he says, "Eden, baby, Eden."

He kisses me on the check, grabs his iPod, and we get out of the car. Opening the trunk, he pulls out a big red beach blanket and what looks like a new sleek iPod docking station. "Come on, we gotta get a move on. I don't want you getting in trouble with Mommy."

"I don't care if I'm late or not," I announce as I follow him toward a line of trees.

"Don't do that. 'Sides, I got a few people coming over tonight," Reid says.

"Can I—"

"Some of my friends, well, they're not so cool. I want to protect you," he says.

"Protect me?" I ask, but Reid doesn't answer. I decide this is my chance to catch both Vic and Kate in their lies. "Reid, how do you get so much money to buy—"

His green eyes flash anger to stop my words, but in seconds, his smile returns. "You ever see that movie *The Godfather?*"

"I guess, why?"

"The best line is when Scarface says to his wife: 'Don't ask me about my business.'"

"Sorry," I mumble.

"Come on," Reid says as he pushes through a hole in the wire fence. I follow behind as we cut through some trees, emerging on a beautiful, sandy, and totally deserted lake beach.

"Reid, this is beautiful," I gush.

"This is my place." Reid lays the towel on the sand and we lie down on it. He pulls out a joint from his cutoffs, then hands me his lighter. I light the joint for him, and he leans back as he inhales. Resting my head on his chest, he asks, "Sure you don't want some?"

"No. That's okay, right?" I ask softly.

"Good shit, but that's cool," he says. "Do whatever you want."

"I am," I whisper as I try to press myself even closer. I can't hear his heart over the sound of the music he's put on, but I can imagine. Just like I imagine this spot and this sunset are somehow just for us.

"You about ready to dive in?" Reid says as he takes another hit.

It's strange, but I'm feeling nervous, so I say, "Let me try that."

He puts the joint on my lips, and I inhale. I've seen Reid and his friends get high often enough, so I know you're supposed to hold the smoke in for the full effect, but I still cough like some wannabe.

"I told you this was good shit," he says, laughing. We sit in silence as we share the joint and take in the sunset. Finally, I get up the nerve to ask, "Do you think I'm beautiful?"

"Where's this coming from?" is his non-answer. I don't say anything, hoping my silence will force him to respond. Finally he says, "Like this sunset, baby."

"Really?" I say, turning to face him.

Reid doesn't say anything; instead, he finishes the joint and moves out from under me. He goes toward the water, then waves for me to join him. With the water lapping at my feet, and his lips and tongue nibbling on my neck, I feel almost faint again.

He takes a step back, then shows that crescent-moon smile again and says, "Really. That's why I want to see more of you."

I pull in a deep breath as he pulls off my tank top, tossing it onto the sand. His hands press gently on my shoulders. My eyes close, my mouth opens, and I believe.

14

SUNDAY, AUGUST 10

"**Why are you being such** a bitch?" I shout at my mom from across the table. After this repeat performance of last Sunday morning's fight, I wonder why she's not asking me the same.

"Reap and sow, baby, reap and sow," is Mom's answer. We've spent another morning at church. Carl came with us, but by noon, he was already back asleep. He's trying to be nicer to Mom and pay some attention to me, but it's hard for him to break old habits. Except for church, Sunday is like any other day for Carl: drinking, sleeping, and softball. Every day's the weekend in his life. No wonder I don't like him. I'm trying to do everything I can to act like an adult; he's an adult acting like he's fifteen. We both want the life that the other one lives.

"I can't stand it here!" I shout, pushing away my half-eaten Halo Burger in anger.

"You shouldn't have lied about Evan, and I want to know about this other boy," she says. I notice that our argument isn't affecting her appetite. She's eating more than usual, which means Carl will be around for a while. Clearly Mom's not working on returning to her date weight.

"This is not fair," I say. On the way home from church, she threatened a grounding.

"Get used to it, it's called life," she says, sipping her Diet Coke and reaching for her second cheeseburger from the grease-stained Halo bag. "Are you going to tell me about this young man you've been seeing or will you make me be the bitch and ground you?" she asks.

"We're just spending time together, that's all," I say, looking away.

"Don't lie to me, and don't think I'm that naive. I was fifteen once myself," she says, hiding a smile.

"I'm almost sixteen!"

"And sometimes you almost act like it, but other times, it's like you're six. I don't want you seeing a boy I've haven't met. I don't even know his name. I just can't approve."

"You don't get to say."

"Yes, I do, I'm your mother," she shoots back. "I'm the adult, although you forget that!"

"Then act like one!" I shout, leaping up from the table.

"You come back here!" she yells at me. I don't run for the door outside; instead I open Mom's bedroom door. Carl's fat, hairy naked ass is aimed right at us, while his fingers seem to be pointing at the nine empty beer cans near the bed. There was enough shouting from their bedroom to raise the dead last night. Mom's not bruised, but her voice is raw. It was only a matter of time. Carl's patience is too thin, Mom's will is too weak, and beer is far too available.

"Who are you to give me advice on men?" I hiss. I'd love to slam the door but I definitely don't want to wake Carl, so I head toward my room.

My mom follows me, saying, "Watch your mouth!"

"Why don't you finally use yours?" I turn on my heel. Standing in the doorway, on the threshold between my room and my mother's, I whisper, "Tell him to leave."

"So help me," she says through a clenched jaw. Although her various boyfriends have slapped me in the past, Mom never has. I push my chin out, half daring half begging her.

"Help you? You're helpless!" This fight about Carl is our own burning circle of hell. "Tell him to leave," I say, softly now.

My mom walks past me, into my room. She sits on the floor next to my bed, then motions for me to join her.

"I can't, Danielle, I can't," she says.

"Why not, Mom? Do you love him that much?"

"I don't love Carl like you think," she says, then wipes her nose, sniffs, and ekes out a smile. "You may think you love this boy, but you don't. You're just young, like I was."

"But Mom, you don't understand."

"No, Danielle, you don't understand love, or men, and maybe I don't either. But I know a few things. I wish you could just believe what I say, but life doesn't work that way. You have to learn most lessons the hard way."

"But Reid—" I shut my mouth, but too late. I've revealed the secret name.

She pulls in a deep breath and puts her head on my shoulder.

"Danielle, baby, it's easy to find men who need you, like Carl needs me. And you'll always find boys who want you, like Evan or this Reid character. But—" She stops, then hugs me like she's trying to pull me back into her body and says, "But the hard thing is finding someone who really loves you for you, and will be true forever."

"But Reid—," I start again.

"And the only people who are going to do that, baby, are your family," she says, trying to smile. "I messed things up with my mom so much; I don't want that to happen between you and me."

"Then stop pushing me about Reid and I'll shut up about Carl," I tell her.

"Okay," she says after a long pause. We spit shake, declaring a truce in our ongoing war.

"I want you home before ten tonight, agreed?" Mom says as I walk toward the door.

"Sure thing," I say, and even give her an overdue big hug. In the other room, Carl's stirring, and I wish I could take Mom with me as I leave.

"Love you, Danny baby, special lady," she says, like she used to when I was little.

"I know, Mom," I say, unable and unwilling to give her an "I love you" in return.

"Promise me one thing," she says, as serious as my mom can sound.

"What?"

"Don't change your life for just any boy. It's a mistake." She stares at me. It seems like she wants to say more, but I can tell it's too hard. What she doesn't know is that unlike Carl, Mitch, or her loser parade, Reid's a winner. What she can't accept is how much my sad, lonely life needed changing and how Reid's making that possible. Mom wants me to still be her dependent passenger, but I'm driving without her now.

.   .   .

"What are you doing here?" Reid asks. I know he told me not to come over, but it's an emergency and only he can save me. I called and called, but he didn't answer, so I took the risk because I need him—just like he said he needed me. He comes to the door after twenty hard knocks. I don't see his mom's truck parked out front, so I figure it's safe. He's staring blankly at me.

I'm feeling confused. Just riding over to Reid's on my bike made me feel lighter than ever before, even going up the steep hill of Maple Road. I felt like I was coasting.

I try to retain my smile in the face of his dismissive frown, then say, "I just thought—"

He cuts me off not with a tender kiss, but with a harsh tone. "It's not a good time."

"I'm sorry, Reid," I say, actually hanging my head in shame.

"Look at me, Danielle," Reid says, then puts his hand on my shoulder. "I have to go."

"What's going on?" I ask.

"My mom," he mumbles. "She's finishing a week-long drinking vacation. Stay away."

"I'm so sorry," I start to say, but he shuts the door in my face.

. . .

I call Ashley and she invites me right over. I pedal as fast as I can, sweating in the sweltering August heat. I wish she was still dog sitting for her neighbors so I'd have an opportunity to jump into the pool and cool down.

"Hey, is Ashley home?" I ask her father when he answers the door.

"Danielle, how have you been? We've missed you like a big front tooth," he says. He's so strange. No wonder Ashley's embarrassed to be seen with him in public.

"Is she here?" I ask. I like Ashley's parents, but even after years of spending time at their house, sometimes I still feel like they're space aliens pretending to be human parents.

"In her room reading, of course," he says, then invites me in. Like magic, Ashley's mother appears with two big glasses of iced tea.

"Here you go!" she says. "Would you mind delivering this to the princess?"

I laugh, but it's kinda true: sometimes they treat her more like a princess than a daughter.

"Hey, Ash, it's Danny," I say as I open her door.

Ashley isn't lying on her bed reading, but instead is sitting in front of her computer. I can't help but take a quick glance at the screen. There's a map of the northeastern part of Michigan, but I can't see any more before she turns off the monitor.

"Planning a trip?" I ask as I hand her the iced tea.

"What do you mean?" she says. She's moved over to her bed, while I sit in the chair by her desk.

"You know," I say, and I click the computer screen back on. Driving directions from Flint to Tawas.

"That's private," she says, setting down her glass.

"I didn't think best friends had secrets," I reply.

She sits back in bed, then takes a deep breath. "Sorry, touchy subject." I click the screen off.

"Who do you know there?" I ask.

She pauses, taking a long sip of tea. "Nobody. We just used to vacation there, that's all."

"Okay," I say, unwilling to confront her about this lie. After I learned she'd lied to me when I spoke with her father, I'd looked up some information about Tawas. It didn't seem like the kind of place her parents would vacation. They normally took Ashley to exciting places like New York or Toronto, not some small town on the shore of Lake Huron. Tawas used to be kind of a nice place, but times got tough: now it's more like run-down Flint than rich Traverse City.

"So how's Reid?" she asks, not looking me in the eye.

"Why do you ask?" I could tell from her tone that there was no point in lying to her.

"I called your house and your mom said you'd left. You weren't here, so I figured you were there, right?"

"Right," I say, taking a deep breath.

"What's wrong?"

I tell Ashley about how Reid wouldn't let me come into the house, but she doesn't seem the least bit upset. Instead she says casually, "I've been talking to Evan about Reid."

"Really?" This proves my conspiracy theory. I don't need to smoke pot to be paranoid.

"And Evan's been talking to his brother Vic," she continues.

"Vic's a loser." I let Reid's words fall out of my mouth.

Ashley pushes her hair out of her eyes, then glares back at me. "Maybe so, but he cares about you. Evan cares about you. I care about you. But all you seem to care about is Reid."

"Don't turn into my mother."

"He's playing you," Ashley says, trying not to sound too smug. "Trust me on this. I knew people like Reid."

"Name one!" As far as I know, I'm Ashley's only close friend. She never talks much about her life before her parents moved to Flint, or even before we met in ninth grade.

"This isn't about me, it's about you," she counters. "He's evil, Danielle."

"Please, Ashley." I sigh, then treat her to an eye roll she can admire. "This isn't some fantasy novel with good versus evil. This is real life. You should try living in it sometime."

"Again, you don't know what you're talking about," she says. "I'm scared for you."

"I can take care of myself," I reassure her.

"He's twisting you," Ashley says. "You have to trust me."

"I don't believe you," I say.

"You don't know anything about him, really, do you?" She sits up in bed, then grabs my hands. "Just because you love someone, or they love you, doesn't mean there are no secrets."

"He loves me," I tell her, pride busting my heart.

"Why aren't you with him now?" she asks. "Why do you spend so little time with him?"

"He isn't able to see me for a while. Besides, he's really busy."

"Interesting," Ashley says, holding my hands tighter.

"What does that mean?" I try to pull my hands away, but she's holding on.

"Oh, Danielle, don't you know?" she asks softly.

"Know what?"

"Reid's just using you. You *must* know that," she says, squeezing my hands tighter still.

"You're just saying that because you're jealous of the time I do spend with him." I free my hands, then move from Ashley's soft bed back to her hard chair.

"Maybe," Ashley says. "And when is that time?"

"Whenever he can," I answer.

"So, you only see him when he wants it," Ashley says. "And if you do what you just did, dropping in on him, what happens?"

"I don't know what you mean," I lie to her face. I *had* dropped in on Reid a couple of other times, and he did then exactly what he just did: sent me away.

"You said you don't go over there much anymore when other people are there, right?"

"That's because he just wants to spend time alone with me," I tell her.

"Like I said, you're being played."

"What makes you so fucking smart all of a sudden?" I shoot back.

"Maybe I'm not smart," she answers, "or maybe I'm just not blindly in love with Reid."

"You're lying," say I, Danielle the Denier.

"I wouldn't lie to you, Danielle," she says softly.

I turn away, then click on the computer screen again. "You're lying about this, I know it."

"Don't turn this back on me," she snaps. "I'm just trying to help you."

"Lying to me isn't helping."

She moves to the edge of the bed. Her arms reach out to me. "I'm just trying to protect you from getting hurt, just like I tried to protect your mom from Carl."

"Reid isn't going to hurt me like that," I tell her. "I trust him."

"And that's the problem," she continues. "Why won't you believe me?"

"Because you're just telling me lies," I insist. I move to sit next to her.

"You won't believe me no matter what I say, will you?"

"No!"

There's silence except for the sound of both of us breathing heavily. "Then I'll prove it."

"How?" I ask. Ashley closes her eyes and goes silent again. I try to speak, but she shushes me, putting her finger against my lips.

"Just let me think," she says, then she leaves the bed and walks over to her desk. She opens her purse and pulls out a hairbrush. Handing the brush to me, she sits on the floor at my feet.

"You know what my best memory of being a child is?" she asks as I start brushing her hair.

"What are you talking about?" I ask, confused by this out-of-place question.

"This," she says. Then she makes a sound like she's covering up crying by laughing. We're silent again, except for the sound of the brush making its way through Ashley's hair. Finally, she says, "I can prove I'm right, if you'll trust me."

"Prove what?"

"Prove I'm your best friend forever and you can trust me no matter what." Ashley stands up to hug me tight, then whispers, "And prove I'm right about Reid."

"How are you going to do that?"

"We'll catch him cheating on you."

"Cheating? With who?"

"Me," is all she says. I shake my head in confusion.

"With my boyfriend?"

"If tempted, I know he'd cheat on you," she says. "I don't want Reid, you know that?"

"I know." There are things I don't know about Ashley, but her loyalty I never question.

"Let me ask you something. Has he ever said he was sorry for what happened before?" I shake my head. "Has he ever apologized to you, or to anyone that you've heard?"

"Why are you asking me these questions?" I ask, distracting myself from giving a real answer.

"I knew people like that," she sputters. She's as near tears as I've ever seen her.

"Like what?" I ask.

"You know right from wrong. You feel bad if you hurt someone. Reid can't."

"Yes, he can!"

"No, Danny, he can't," Ashley says. "Reid's not cool. He's just got no conscience."

"What are you saying?" I'm grabbing on to her hands, which are shaking as badly as mine.

"Reid is a sociopath," Ashley says. Her bone-chilling words are: "I saw it, Danny, I saw it in his snake-charmer eyes. He's dead inside. If you're not careful, he's going to destroy you."

15

WEDNESDAY AFTERNOON, AUGUST 13

"Is Danielle here?" Ashley says when Reid answers his door.

I try not to breathe too heavily, so Reid won't hear me. Ashley's phone is on, at the top of her open purse. My phone is jammed against my ear. The cell crackles like fire against my face.

"No, she's not," Reid answers. I don't want to be here. I don't want to go through with this, but Ashley swears it's the only way to convince me that Reid is what she says he is. I finally gave in after days of her wearing me down. I want to prove her wrong and slay all my doubts. Now Ashley's at Reid's front door, while I'm in the alley listening to their conversation.

"Well, I need to talk with her," Ashley says, sounding upset, pretending to cry.

"Oh yeah, you're her friend."

"Ashley."

"We met the day I drove you to the library, right?" he asks, then there's an awkward silence as Reid doesn't ask why Ashley needs to talk with me.

"We had a big fight, and now she's missing," she says, making the lie sound like solid truth.

"She's not over here," Reid says, sounding almost bored.

"I'm really worried," Ashley says through more fake tears. "It was a big fight."

"Over what?"

"Over you."

"Me?" Reid says. I just know he's breaking out that special smile of his for her.

"You." I imagine her fingers adjusting the strap of the tight white top I picked out. I'm wondering if Reid's looking at her like he looks at me.

"You wanna come inside, it's hot as a jungle out there," he suggests. I hear Ashley follow him into the house. From the number of steps, they're probably in the living room.

"Thanks, it's cooler in here," she says. I imagine her tossing her hair back out of her eyes.

"Cooler down the basement," Reid adds. "Come on down, I'll get you a beer."

"That would be great, thanks," Ashley lies. I tell myself everything she says is a lie; I wonder if it's the same with everything Reid's told me. I listen to them walk down the basement stairs, and I imagine them sitting on the couch by the big-screen TV.

"You're fighting about me?" Reid asks over the sound of beer bottles being opened.

"Sorry, I shouldn't have come over here," Ashley announces. It sounds like she's drinking, but strangely I don't hear her gag like I did my first time or pronounce it "grotesque."

"So what's the problem?"

"Umm, I don't know how to say this," Ashley says. She's talking softer now; it's getting harder to hear, especially over the increased pounding of my heart.

It sounds like Reid whispers, "You can say whatever you want."

"You see, this is so embarrassing. You don't even know me."

"My mistake," he says, then laughs. "I guess I'm allowed to make one."

Ashley giggles the kind of giggle we'd make fun of other girls at school for doing when some boy said something only slightly funny. "Well, *I* made one coming here."

"What do you mean?" he asks.

"We fought because I told Danielle how I've thought about you ever since we first came over here. But when I saw you that day, I knew." Ashley lets the lies rush out of her.

"Knew what?"

"Knew I couldn't stop thinking about you," Ashley says, followed by a long silence, which I wait for Reid to fill by saying something like, "Wow, that's nice but, you see, Danielle is my girlfriend," or "You'd better leave now," or anything. But there's just quiet.

"I could tell when I saw you the other day," he says at last. "The way you stared at me."

"I could tell in your eyes exactly who you were." Ashley's breathing heavy.

"You wanna smoke a joint?" Reid says, I think. He's back to almost whispering.

Another long pause. "That's not what I want in my mouth." Ashley lets the bold words fall.

"Cool."

"No, Reid, cold as hell," she says. I even gave her the words to say.

"You are very sexy," he purrs. No doubt he's also pawing her. "From what I can see."

I hear rustling sounds over the echo of my breaking heart.

"Very hot, very sexy," he says, then I hear what sounds like a kiss. It goes on for a while, the longest moment of my life. It ends when Reid finally says, "Especially your mouth."

More rustling sounds, then the sound of a beer bottle being set down on a table. More moaning and slurping. And now the jingle of a belt buckle being undone, followed by my boyfriend Reid saying to my best friend forever Ashley, "Why don't you show me that sexy mouth in action?"

· · ·

"I hate you!" I shout at Reid's unshaven face. I wanted to yell it into the cell as soon as I'd heard his words and deeds. Shout it as I let myself in through the back door. Scream it as I got to the top of the basement stairs. But I waited. I waited until I saw him sitting on the sofa with his pants around his ankles, while Ashley assumed my usual position.

"Hey, wait," Reid says as he starts pulling up his pants.

"I hate you!" I shout again, and again, and again.

"This was all her idea!" He points at Ashley.

"You're right, it was," Ashley says, taking the cell phone out of her purse.

"This is bullshit!" he shouts, then tries to cool down. "Danielle, just wait. Look at me."

"I've already seen enough of you!" I scream at him. "How could you do this to me?"

Reid doesn't say anything. He doesn't apologize. He doesn't care. Ashley was right.

"I'm your girlfriend," I cry out.

"You were never *my* girlfriend," Reid says like he's spitting in my face. "You were *a* girlfriend."

"Fuck you, Reid!" I shout as I race up the stairs. I hear Ashley's steps behind me; I don't hear Reid's. I wonder if he heard my tears as I ran through his house, or the sound of the front door as I slammed it loud enough to shake the windows. But mostly, I wonder if he heard me lifting the keys to his Viper off the kitchen table.

16

WEDNESDAY EVENING, AUGUST 13

I'm fifteen years old and I'm driving a stolen car. Ashley, my best friend forever, sits beside me. Despite my long light-brown hair, I'm the Goldilocks of the interstate: not too slow, not too fast. The speed is just right to avoid attention, while taking us far away from Flint, from family, from friends, and from a summer filled with faithlessness.

I don't want a stolen car; what I need is a time machine to reverse the past two months of my life. Before all this, if someone was doing a word association game and said my name—Danielle Griffin—the word "normal" would have been the right answer. Since I kept my home life hidden from most people, I was just another under-the-radar sophomore at Carmen High School. I used to read books and think, "Why couldn't something exciting happen to me?" But I'd trade all the turmoil of the past two months in a second to have my boring loveless life back.

And it is love, or something like it, that has us heading north on I-75 through the hot and muggy August Michigan air. I'm not sure how any of this will end, but for now, I'm driving a stolen car on a steamy starless night, wishing I could vanish into the black void.

• • •

"Is Evan there?" I say, as serious as possible. I'm falling apart inside, which I hide by trying to keep it together on the outside. We're parked at a rest stop on I-75, north of Flint. All my focus has been on the road, not my ravaged soul.

"Hey, Danielle, is everything all right?" Vic answers.

"I just need to talk to Evan."

"Just a second," Vic says, then I hear him yell Evan's name. Trucks pull in and out of the rest stop as I wait.

"Danielle, what's wrong?" Evan says when he comes on the line. I notice Vic doesn't hang up, and I don't make an issue out of it.

"Do you have any money?" I ask softly. We started out straight from Reid's house at Ashley's suggestion, so we've got no clothes, no food, no money, and no plans.

"What's wrong?" he repeats.

"Evan, are you my friend?" I ask.

"Well, that's your choice."

"Be serious, please!"

"Of course, Danielle, I'm your friend."

"Then I need money," I say. "I don't have time to explain right now, but I will later. I'll tell you the whole story, but right now, if you're my friend, you'll bring us some cash."

"Us?" Evan asks.

"Ashley's with me," I tell him. "Can you get here quickly?"

"My mom has the car, so—"

Vic interrupts. "We'll take the junker. It's got a few miles left in it. Where are you?"

I give him the location, trying to sound a lot calmer than I am.

"How the hell did you get all the way up there?" Evan asks.

"I've stolen a car," I say, but before Evan can say anything, Vic jumps back in.

"What'd you boost?" Vic asks.

"A red Dodge Viper," I say, and I swear I can hear Vic smile through the phone.

"Sweet ride," Vic says. "Think he'll miss it?"

"More than he'll miss me," I say. Then I hang up.

"Where should we go?" I ask Ashley. We've got the windows rolled down as I smoke the last of Reid's Newports. I need his taste in my mouth one last time to make all of this real.

"Let's just keep driving north, okay?" she says softly. I nod, wondering if this trip north will finally help me color in Ashley's life and uncover the secrets I sense she's been hiding from me.

"Sounds like a plan," I say, then start to laugh so I don't cry. Ashley's parents and Mom will be looking for us. I'm not sure about Reid. I'm not sure about anything anymore, except that Reid won't call the police. As Vic once told me, the best person to steal from is another thief.

We talk some more, or rather I talk and Ashley listens. I pour out my heart and my hurt and my hate, all of them mixed up. Ashley never says I told you so, instead she just listens.

After about an hour, Vic and Evan finally show up in the junker. They park next to us. Vic's laughing, but Evan looks confused.

Vic turns the car around and parks. Evan gets out and walks over while Vic stays behind. "What kind of trouble have you gotten yourself into?" Evan asks.

"I'll get myself out of it," I say, putting out my hand. He hands me a wad of cash, then I kiss him on the cheek. "Like the Beatles say, 'I'll get by with a little help from my friends.'"

He doesn't try to turn the kiss into anything else. Instead, he looks down at the ground in front of us, then says all serious, "Danielle, just tell me what's going on. Tell me how I can help."

"I'll be okay." I'm lying to him, because I can't explain how angry and afraid I am right now.

"I'm worried about you," he says softly.

"Evan, I'm sorry," I say just as softly. I'm speaking to Evan, but I'm looking over at Vic. I wish he could hear my words too when I say, "I haven't been very nice to you."

Evan shrugs his shoulders, then says, "Don't worry, everything's okay between us. Call me when you get back."

I wave goodbye as Evan climbs back into Vic's junker. I notice Vic isn't in the car anymore; he's kneeling behind the Viper. Ashley and I get out and walk behind the car.

"What are you doing?" Ashley asks.

"Switching plates," Vic says. "I snagged 'em off a rental car at the airport."

"What?" I ask.

"Look, if Reid reports his car stolen, they'll be looking for his plates," Vic says. "So, we'll just put these plates on, and nobody knows nothing for a while. It'll buy you some time."

"You're a genius," I say, patting Vic on the shoulder.

"No, my brother's the genius," Vic says. "I'm just a thief."

"An ex-thief," I correct him.

He laughs, then heads back to his car as Ashley and I climb back into Reid's Viper on our way north.

I merge onto the interstate, feeling more confident. I've turned on the radio, and I have even managed to find my smile.

"What are you thinking about?" Ashley asks.

"How sweet Evan is," I tell her.

"There are two kinds of people in this world; don't you know that by now?" She settles back in her seat like the philosopher queen on her throne. "There's people like Reid who take, and there's people like Evan who give."

"I don't know how Evan could still like me and say everything was okay."

"You'd be amazed what you can forgive in this world," Ashley says.

"I guess," I mutter.

"You don't believe me, do you?" she asks. Without taking my eyes off the road, I give a big headshake. "I can prove *that* to you as well."

"How's that?" I ask.

"Just keep driving north." She's looking at the map that now rests in her lap.

"To Tawas?" I ask. She nods and I decide I'm going to be a person who takes, and Ashley's going to be a person who finally gives me an answer.

"So, what's there?" I ask her.

"I can't tell you, not yet," Ashley says.

"What did you say to me? 'Best friends forever' isn't just an expression, it's a promise. And the promise is that you tell each other the truth, so how about it?"

"I can't."

"Ashley, you can do anything," I tell her. "You proved that today."

"I guess," she mumbles.

"You can trust me," I say. "I think I proved that today as well."

"That's true," she says, trying not to smile.

"So why are we driving north?" I continue. "What's in Tawas?"

Ashley's silent for a while, but I swear I hear her heart beating faster. "I'm going to prove one more thing to you," she finally says.

"What's that?"

She looks out the window into the starless night. Her voice sounds broken when she says, "Something real important that I told you once: you can forgive a person for anything if you love them enough."

. . .

"Danielle, where are you?" Mom manages to mix all of the anger, fear, and worry that are running through her body into just four words.

"I can't tell you," I say. We've driven another seventy miles or so, but Ashley hasn't said another word after her last oracle pronouncement. She's not sleeping; she's just not speaking.

"What are you talking about?" Mom asks. I look at the clock in the car. I'm past late. I've had the cell turned off just in case Reid called. Actually, I turned it off so I wouldn't know that he *wasn't* calling. When I finally turn it on, all my messages are from Mom, none from Reid.

"Mom," I say, trying to stay calm, "you know how I always say you have to trust me?"

"All the time."

"This time I mean it. I'm not coming home tonight. Ashley and I are okay. Things are just complicated, but you have to trust me that we're both okay."

"Where are you?"

"Mom, I'm okay. I don't want to say anything else. Don't worry."

"Don't worry! How can you say that?" she says, almost

hysterical. "You're three hours late coming home and you won't tell me where you are. Of course I'm worried."

"Mom, please, I just need some time," I tell her calmly, but she's still anxious.

"I'm coming to get you," she announces. "I'll have Carl call the police. I'll—"

"Mom, no. You can't do that. I have to work this out on my own."

"Work what out?"

"Reid and I broke up," I tell her. "Please don't say 'I told you so' or anything, just tell me one thing."

"What's that?"

"Just tell me you love me no matter what."

Mom pauses, takes a deep breath. I think I hear a smoke being lit. "Of course I do, Danny. I'll love you no matter what. That's why I'm so worried about you."

"I'll be home tomorrow, maybe the next day," I tell her. I'm not lying; I don't know what we're going to do. About the only thing I know is that I'll never, ever see Reid again.

"Promise me you'll call me again," Mom says. "Promise me everything is all right."

"Promise," I tell her. "Can you do something for me?"

"Baby, what do you need?" Mom says.

"Ashley's with me. Can you tell her parents that she's okay?"

"Why can't she tell them herself?" Mom asks with concern, not anger. I look over at Ashley and she's still staring out the window, like she's going into one of her trance-like states.

"It's all complicated, Mom, but please, please just let them know."

"Where are the two of you? They'll want to know."

I tap Ashley on the shoulder and she turns around, her eyes red. "My mom needs to know where we're going. She has to tell your parents something."

"Tell her to just tell them that we're looking for someone," Ashley says.

"Who's that?" I ask.

She takes a deep breath, turns away from me again, and says, "My mother."

"Your mother?" I try to get her to talk, but she just keeps staring out the window.

. . .

I'm still following the signs north, but it's getting harder. I'm exhausted, not just from having to super-concentrate on driving, but from all the day's events, especially Ashley's last statement.

"I need to sleep," I tell her as I follow the road into Tawas. "I'm pulling over."

"No, we need to find a motel," she says.

"I don't think we could get a room on our own," I confess. "Even if we could, Evan didn't give us that much money. No, we'll just sleep in the car."

"No! Danielle, I won't sleep in the car." She's not talking, she's shrieking.

"But Ashley, we don't—"

"I won't do it," she says, then points at a road sign. "There used to be a cheap motel just on the other side of downtown. Please, let's just go there."

I want to ask her how she knows about the motel. I need to ask her what she meant about looking for her mom. But mostly I want and need to sleep, while I sense Ashley needs time.

Ashley uses the little bit of makeup she has in her purse to make herself look older than her sixteen years. She goes into the motel office and returns a few minutes later with a key. I park the car near the back of the lot, which is mostly full of semitrucks. We stumble toward the room like two lost travelers through the muggy midnight air.

The place is pretty dirty, but I don't care. I go to the bathroom first. By the time Ashley comes out, I'm lying faceup, staring at the ugly off-white cracked ceiling. It's hard to even hear myself breathe over the loud fan of the air conditioner and the louder TV in the room next door. I try to turn the fan off, but the knob is broken. Like the town outside, this motel's seen better times.

Ashley sits on the edge of my bed, pulling her hair away from her face and staring at me.

"I'm sorry I got us into this," I tell her.

"It's not your fault," she says, then kicks off her shoes and lies down next to me.

"I should have known. Everybody told me, but..." I stop, waiting for the I-told-you-so moment, but it doesn't come.

"Remember what I told you at the start of the summer?" she asks. I shake my head. "You can't tell people stuff, you have to show them. Reid had to show you who he really was."

"But I knew, I knew," I say, trying to hold back tears.

"Knew what?"

"Knew he was too old for me. Knew he was too good-looking. Knew that—"

Ashley cuts me off, her voice sharp. "No, it's not that. It's not that at all."

"Then what?"

"That he had no conscience. No guilt or sorrow," she whispers. "I saw it in his eyes."

"How could you know that?" I ask.

She takes a deep breath, then says, "It's complicated. You can't tell anyone."

"Promise," I say as she puts her head on my shoulder, then speaks to the ceiling.

"Those people I live with, they're not my real parents," Ashley starts. "They adopted me when I was eleven. Before that, I was living in foster homes with other rejects, each home worse than the last. Then Peter and Elizabeth came into my life. I did everything I could to get them to hate me, because I didn't think I deserved any better. I didn't just put up a fence around my heart; I loaded it with explosives and barbed wire. I almost destroyed myself."

"Ashley, I didn't know."

"I didn't want you to know that Ashley," she explains. "I

drank, did drugs, everything I hate now. I was so angry that I needed to act out. That's what my therapist helped me recognize."

"I understand so much now," I reassure her, but she just waves it off.

"I'd done more shit by the time we met than any fourteen-year-old should have. But every time, the 'rents kept taking me back, trying their best, loving me. Finally I knew they were real, and that I could have a home again, and something like a normal life, even if I'll never be normal."

"What will you be?"

"I'll just be Ashley."

"Ashley, I didn't know," I repeat.

"I couldn't tell you. I'm so ashamed of who I was and the things I did," Ashley says. "I'm tired of lying to you, to myself. It's too hard, and after everything that happened today, I knew we could really trust each other. So, I'm sorry I lied to you about so many things."

"Like what else?"

"Well, you've known me for two years. For two years I've told you I take piano lessons, but have you ever seen me play the piano? No, I go to *therapy* once a week, but it's not enough. I'm also on medication, anti-depressants, and some other stuff."

I'm just staring. Ashley's hair has fallen over her eyes, but that's not her only mask.

"The therapy helps me understand. My therapist is really smart. She's why I'm always spouting wisdom," she says. "It's all part of processing the pain, anger, and loss in my life."

"But your parents seem—"

"Don't call them my parents," Ashley says. "I had a mother, now I have these people."

"What about your dad?" I ask, but I only get a cold stare in return. It reminds me of the way she stared at Reid the first time she saw him, like her eyes were knives cutting into flesh.

"These people? You sound like you don't love them, but I know you do," I say.

"No, Danielle, I don't love them," she says, as icy cold as the room. "I like them most of the time. I appreciate them, and I respect them, but I don't love them."

"You're just angry," I say. There's this new Ashley in front of me and I'm confused.

"I *can't* love them," she says. "That would be betraying my mom. Can you understand that? Like I said, it's hard, especially since they tell me all the time how much they love me."

"They're not just saying that," I tell her.

"I know, but it's not the same," she says, her teeth chattering. "You can't say it, you have to show it. I came here to show my mom I still love her."

"Do you want to call her?" I ask. "Could we stay with her tonight?"

"I'm so cold," is Ashley's strange non-reply.

"The fan is broken, or I can't figure it out, I'm sorry," I say.

"I'm freezing!"

"Let me take another look at it." I get out of bed, but Ashley grabs my arm.

"Danielle, can I ask you something?" She's whispering again.

"What?"

"Will you forgive Reid?"

I don't even need to think before I say, "No, I can't and I won't." Reid was right, I wasn't his girlfriend, but I wasn't even *a* girlfriend. I was just another victim. I go to sleep tonight as Danielle the Defeated. I can only hope in the morning, when Ashley reconnects with her mom, that I can share her joy—because I feel none tonight.

17

THURSDAY, AUGUST 14

"Ashley, where are you?" I ask, but there's no answer other than the sound of running water. I quickly get dressed, then find some change so I can get a Coke to help myself wake up. When I get back to the room, the water is still running.

"I'll be in the car," I shout through the bathroom door. I snatch the keys, then head outside to let my brain try and absorb all the intense experiences of the past few hours. I find a half-smoked cigarette under the passenger seat. It has lipstick on it; a brown shade of lipstick I don't wear, but Angie does. I turn my phone back on. More missed calls from Mom, Evan, and Ashley's "parents." And one call from Reid, which I return.

"Where's my car, bitch?" Reid shouts at me the second he answers. Before he picked up, part of me hoped against hope that the past twenty-four hours had just been a nightmare. "I said, where the fuck is my Viper?"

"How many?" I reply, holding on to the lipstick-stained cigarette.

"How many what?"

"How many other girls?" I ask. I instantly understand how my mom must feel before Carl hits her: she knows the blow is coming, but something stubborn, proud, and stupid keeps her from backing down.

"How many other girls *what?*" Reid snaps back.

"Did you have sex with?" Acid churns in my stomach as I ask the question.

His laughter is like a needle jabbing into my ear.

"I didn't have sex with you, girl," he chortles. "You just blew me."

I lick my bitter lips but say nothing.

"And you weren't even that good at it," he continues. I turn another cheek. I need his contempt, disrespect, and hatred to keep me away from him forever. "Maybe I should have had Angie or somebody give you lessons. I shouldn't have asked a girl to do a woman's job."

I throw the cigarette out the window, although I think about throwing it under the hood of Reid's car, then running like hell.

"I did take lessons," I say once he stops laughing.

"From who?"

"From Vic," I shoot back. Then I start the car.

"So, he's a faggot as well as a loser." More laughter, more pain, more relief.

"No, Vic taught me how to get rid of a stolen car, one piece at a time," I say slowly over the racing engine. "First, you need the right driving music!"

I can barely hear him shout, "Don't touch my car, bitch" over the Viper's mighty roar and the sound of "Highway to Hell" blasting birds out of the trees.

. . .

"Where to?" I ask Ashley when she finally emerges from the motel room.

"I think I remember," she says, then yawns as she gets into the car.

"You're sure you don't want to call?"

She responds with silence, simply pointing which way I should turn.

"Where did you live?" I ask as we drive slowly through the small town. I can see how maybe once this had been a nice place to live, but now it's filled with boarded-up stores, vacant lots, tons of houses for sale, and more pawnshops than fashion boutiques.

"Mostly here," she says.

"No, I meant where was your house?"

Ashley leans over and taps me on the shoulder, then points to the backseat. "The last year, we mostly lived in Mom's car. We had lived with relatives, at a shelter, but mostly I remember sleeping in the car: Mom in front, me in back, even sometimes in the freezing winter."

I don't say anything. Instead, I use my mathematical mind to add it up: her hatred not just of driving, but of riding in cars, plus her fit last night about needing to find a motel. I look over at Ashley. I've seen or spoken to her almost every day for nearly two years—I've called her my best friend almost as long as I've known her. But I understand now that I'll never really know her, because the life she's telling me about is one I can't begin to imagine living. Most of my life I've been poor, living in dumpy trailer parks, but Ashley's lived like a refugee.

"It's around here someplace," she says after we pull off one of the main roads. The open windows suck in the humid August air, but Ashley looks like she's shivering again, with a coldness in her bones from her childhood that won't depart.

"What happened?" I finally get up the nerve to ask her.

"What do you mean?" she asks, but she's just trying to avoid the question.

"Before I see your mom, could you tell me, what happened? Why were you adopted?"

"We're almost there. Up this road about a mile, then take a right on Church Street," she says, then puts both of her hands over her face.

"We should call your mom. I think we're lost," I say after following her directions. Church Street only goes for about a block before it ends at a set of open iron gates.

"No, this is it," Ashley says, as we both read the sign in front of those gates: St. Mary's Cemetery.

I pull the car off the road. Ashley walks into the cemetery; I follow a few feet behind. I hear the dirt crunching under our feet, and a strange sound coming from Ashley. I see, even from behind, her body shaking like a tall tree in a tornado. I'm just about to rush toward her when she kneels down next to a gravestone. She runs her fingers slowly over the cold marble letters, then speaks without a tear in sight. "I was only five when it started."

"It?" I ask from my standing position.

"OxyContin," she says. "They call it hillbilly heroin."

"Ashley, I'm so sorry," I say, then flash back on her run-in with Carl on the way home from the wedding, when he was yelling about hillbillies.

"It didn't take long; Mom wasn't that strong," Ashley says, her voice wavering. "My mom was like this beautiful flower, but day by day, the petals kept falling away. She lost her job, then her friends, and even her family wouldn't talk to her or help her out."

"Except you," I whisper, lightly touching her shoulder. She puts her hand on top of mine.

"No matter what, she protected me the best she could," Ashley continues, squeezing down on my hand. "I only wish I could have done the same for her."

"What do you mean?" I say, all the while trying not to cry; I've cried so many times in front of Ashley, but now I had to be the strong one. I needed to become Danielle the Defender once again.

"My dad had that same look in his eyes as Reid," she answers.

"What are you talking about?"

"He was a user and abuser. He got Mom hooked, then left us. He'd come back, beat her, and then leave again. Until the next time," Ashley snarls. "He was efficient. Dad did the maximum damage in the minimum amount of time, and I did nothing."

"But you were only a child," I remind her.

"I could have done something, anything," Ashley says. "I couldn't save her."

"Ashley, don't be so hard—"

But she cuts me off. "She sold her clothes, all my toys, everything we owned. But she never sold the car, and she never did anything that put me in danger."

She stops talking, like there are words inside her too heavy to speak.

"Ashley, I—"

"I came home one day from school when I was eight and she was dead on the floor of the trailer we were squatting in." Ashley turns back to touch the gravestone again and sits down on the more brown than green cemetery grass. "The last petal in the wind."

"I don't know what to say."

"There's nothing to say." She puts her hands on both sides of the gravestone. "It wasn't her fault. It was Dad. It was the drugs. It was her love that destroyed us. I've been so angry at her for so long, for abandoning me."

I'm silent, and for almost a minute, so is Ashley.

For all the time I've known her, she stayed strong through every disappointment. She never cried.

Then it happens. Ashley curls up against the gravestone, letting its weight support her. Years of dammed-up tears rush out of her for seconds, minutes, more, pushed forward by screams. Between the screams, I hear her whisper into the marble memorial, "Mommy, I'm gonna be okay now. I forgive you," over and over again.

. . .

"What's going on?" Evan says when I reach him on the phone at work.

"I need one more favor," I say. I'm sitting in the Viper, talking on my cell. Ashley asked me to leave her alone with her mom. She's making peace with her past; now it's my turn.

"So you turned to your *favor*-rite person," Evan says.

"When do you get off work?"

"In about two hours. What's going on now?"

"Is Vic around your house?" I ask.

"Where else is he going to go?" Evan says.

"Can you meet us in a couple of hours at that rest stop again?" I ask. "Both you and Vic."

"What's going on?"

"Well, okay, I need two favors," I say.

"Not thirty-one favors?" Evan cracks. It's not funny, but I laugh to reward the effort.

"First favor is to meet us, and the second"—I pause, then continue—"is to not ask why."

. . .

When Ashley finally comes back to the car, she looks older, and not just because of the dark circles under her eyes. She doesn't say much, other than she's ready to go home. I notice she says "home" and I wonder if she really means it. I know that I do.

We're only waiting in the rest stop for about twenty minutes when Vic and Evan pull up. They're driving their mom's car, and Evan is still in his work clothes: my knight in shining armor is wearing a fugly red uniform, but his smile is cute and inviting.

"You hungry?" he asks, getting out of the car to walk over to us. He's holding bags of burgers and fries, while Vic has a tray full of soft drinks.

"Always," I say as we walk toward one of the picnic tables.

As we're eating, Evan interrupts with his usual jokes and puns, but fails in his attempt to get me to squirt Coke through my nose. Whenever I laugh, he looks at me so kindly. Maybe because he's looking me in the eyes for a change, he seems different. Or maybe it's me.

"Here's your money back." I take the unspent cash and hand it to Evan.

"It's his," Evan says, pointing at Vic.

"Thanks," I say, but no doubt the worry shows as I ask, "Where did you get this?"

"I liquidated some remaining assets from my portfolio," Vic says, then winks.

"What?" Ashley asks.

"I waited until Reid wasn't home, busted in, stole back a bunch of shit I stole for him, then pawned it all over Flint, Saginaw, and Bay City. I figure he owes me, and there's nothing he can do to me now because I'm not one of his flunkies anymore." Vic laughs, but then turns all serious talking right at Evan. "That's it, I'm done."

"You've said that before," Evan says, sounding more sad than angry.

"I mean it, I'm done," Vic says, then looks at me. "You believe me, Danielle, right?"

"Yeah, I do," I say to Vic, but I'm looking at Evan. "You gotta have a little faith."

"I wish I had enough bills left to get some new wheels. Then I'd be so gone," Vic says.

"Here," I say to Vic as I flip him the keys to the Viper.

"What are you doing?" Evan asks.

"Evan, I'm giving you a chance to give me and Ashley a ride home," I say.

"Are you sure?" Vic asks.

"Positive," I tell him and I get a big hug from him in return.

Vic squeezes the keys, like a charm. "Finally, some good luck."

"Tell us where to send your stuff," Evan says, but Vic shakes his head.

"There's nothing in Flint I want or need," Vic replies. "I'm gonna start fresh." He pulls Evan aside, hugs him, and whispers something in his ear. He starts toward the Viper but stops when I yell after him.

I run to catch him, then say, "You know that old song you told me about the other day?"

"Which one?" Vic asks, looking puzzled.

"The one about how even losers get lucky sometimes," I say, then whisper, "Well, Vic, maybe this isn't luck, and you and Evan for sure aren't losers."

I'd like to think Vic is still smiling at what I said as he roars out of the rest stop driving Reid's Viper not just across the county line, but into the next and best part of his life.

· · ·

"Call me later, okay?" Ashley says as Evan pulls up in front of her house. It's the first thing she's said in about an hour. She sat in silence, staring out the window, and we just let her be. I'd given her the front seat next to Evan, even though I wanted to be next to him. I vowed that when I start driving—legally, that is—I'll never make Ashley sit in the backseat again.

"Is she okay?" Evan asks as soon as Ashley climbs out of the car.

"She'll be okay," I reply, hoping my confidence in her turns into strength.

Waving me to come into the front, Evan says, "How about you, Danielle?"

"I think I'm going to be okay too," I answer, quickly moving out of the backseat. Then we drive away; Evan keeps both hands on the wheel, while I keep both eyes on him.

"Really?" Evan says.

"Well, I guess it depends," I say, moving closer to him.

"On what?"

"I relish the chance to ketchup with an old friend," I say, trying not to laugh.

"That's quite the pickle," he replies. "Where does this friend work?"

"Halo Burger," I tell him.

"He must be an angel," Evan cracks, and I laugh. I've danced with the devil, or something like it, but all along I've had this adoring if somewhat annoying angel watching over me. The things we want are always so far out of reach, while the things we need can be so close if we'd just listen to our better intentions.

I get out of the car quickly at my house. I don't want to ruin the smooth, friendly exchanges of the last few minutes with an awkward moment at my front door. I give Evan the "I'll call you" sign instead of a kiss. He smiles, not a crescent moon, but definitely sincere.

· · ·

There's a note from Mom on the table to call her at work. I try her once, but she's too busy to say much other than how glad she is that I'm home. She sounds more relieved than angry, so forgiveness may follow. I fall down on my bed, bone-tired from the past few days.

I'm not sure how long I'd slept when I hear a loud banging at the front door. Mom mentioned Carl had a softball game, which probably turned into a beer-drinking contest. I try ignoring the pounding, but it's too loud. I curse Carl's name and go to the front door.

Reid is standing on the three-step porch, with Angie sitting in a black Mustang Cobra behind him. I crack open the door, but first put on the chain lock.

"Where's my Viper?" Reid says, almost ripping the screen off the hinge.

"It's gone," I say.

"You bitch," he hisses.

"How does it feel to lose something you love?" I shout back at him.

"You fat ugly bitch," he says, kicking at the door. "You're in for it."

"What are you going to do, Reid?" I say as I push against the door, which seems ready to give.

His mouth stays quiet, while his foot continues to kick the door. I take a quick look at the phone, and try to figure how quickly I can get it and dial 911 before he knocks anything down. "I'll be happy to call the police if you want, Reid!" He answers with another kick.

"Fuck you, Danielle!" Reid shouts, then kicks the door so hard the wood splinters.

"No, fuck you!" I hear Carl's voice from the other side of the door, followed by loud noises. After about a minute, I hear Carl shout, "Danny, you okay?"

I open the door to see Carl standing at the foot of the porch. He's swinging his softball bat over his head like a helicopter blade. Reid's on the ground, holding his left leg.

"Unless you want some more of this, you'll get out of here now. And don't fucking come back here or I'll do worse!"

Carl shouts at Reid. Reid stares at me, at Carl, and then at Angie.

"Reid, are you hurt?" Angie asks, shooting an angry glare at me.

"Stay in the car," he shouts. "Let's get the fuck out of here."

Reid crawls back into the car, pushing himself behind the wheel.

"You're sure you're okay?" Carl asks as we both watch Reid's taillights disappear.

"Thanks, Carl," I say, avoiding his eyes.

"Well, watch yourself," Carl says, pointing the bat at me.

I pause, then reach out to take the bat from him, asking, "Why did you do it?"

"Do what?" he asks, handing me the softball bat, his temporary sword of honor.

"Protect me," I mumble.

"You're part of my family." Carl moves closer to me, but doesn't reach out with his arms; his actions have already said more than his words, even as he asks, "What's going on?"

"It's complicated," I say. And then, with a rare smile aimed at Carl, I add, "A lot like families."